DRAGON GUARD WARRIOR

ALSO BY ALICIA MONTGOMERY

THE TRUE MATES SERIES

Fated Mates

Blood Moon

Romancing the Alpha

Witch's Mate

Taming the Beast

Tempted by the Wolf

THE LONE WOLF DEFENDERS SERIES

Killian's Secret

Loving Quinn

All for Connor

THE TRUE MATES STANDALONE NOVELS

Holly Jolly Lycan Christmas

A Mate for Jackson: Bad Alpha Dads

TRUE MATES GENERATIONS

A Twist of Fate

Claiming the Alpha

Alpha Ascending

A Witch in Time
Highland Wolf
Daughter of the Dragon
Shadow Wolf
A Touch of Magic
Heart of the Wolf

The Blackstone Mountain Series

The Blackstone Dragon Heir
The Blackstone Bad Dragon
The Blackstone Bear
The Blackstone Wolf
The Blackstone Lion
The Blackstone She-Wolf
The Blackstone She-Bear
The Blackstone She-Dragon

Blackstone Rangers Series

Blackstone Ranger Chief
Blackstone Ranger Charmer
Blackstone Ranger Hero
Blackstone Ranger Rogue
Blackstone Ranger Guardian
Blackstone Ranger Scrooge

Dragon guard of the Northern Isles

Dragon Guard Warrior
Dragon Guard Scholar

This is a work of fiction. Names, characters, businesses, places, events, locales, and incidents are either the products of the author's imagination or used in a fictitious manner. Any resemblance to actual persons, living or dead, or actual events is purely coincidental.

Copyright © 2021 Alicia Montgomery
www.aliciamontgomeryauthor.com
First electronic publication February 2021

Edited by LaVerne Clark
Cover by Jacqueline Sweet
032421

All rights reserved.

DRAGON GUARD WARRIOR

Dragon Guard of the Northern Isles Book 1

ALICIA MONTGOMERY

CHAPTER 1

No matter how many times Poppy Baxter wiped her hands, her palms refused to stay dry. Though she rubbed them down the polyester-blend fabric of her trouser suit repeatedly, sweat would inevitably begin to form on them again, even in the temperature-controlled environment of the Wilfordshire Nanny Staffing Agency waiting room.

She shifted on the leather couch, trying to ignore the other people around her: all young, good-looking women—and one man—groomed and made-up, wearing clothes that probably cost more than what she earned in a week as a primary school teacher. *Used to earn,* she corrected herself. That was the reason she was here, after all.

"Is he yours?"

The question jolted Poppy out of her thoughts, and she quickly glanced beside her where her son, Wesley, had his head bowed down, so deeply engrossed in his book it was as if no one else was in the room.

"Yes, he is," she said to the woman on the settee across from them.

"He's adorable." The woman smiled, got up, smoothing her hands down her wool skirt. Circling around the chrome and glass coffee table, she knelt in front of Wesley. "Hello, poppet. How old are you?"

Wesley's gaze flickered up her, then to Poppy's, before rolling his eyes. "Nine," he replied, then returned to his book.

"Nine going on thirty," Poppy said with a nervous chuckle.

She remained unfazed by Wesley's curtness. "Oh wow, nine years old." She glanced at the book's title. "And you're reading Greek myths and legends already. That's a big book for a boy your age. Which one is your favorite? I bet it's Hercules. Every boy wants to be strong and brave like Hercules."

Without looking up from the pages, Wesley said, "Hercules was an ill-tempered, unstable brute. Why would I want to be like him?"

Her expression only faltered for a moment. "You're so precious." She looked up at Poppy, her face a cheerful mask. "And very smart. I bet you're proud of his ... uh, critical thinking skills. You must be so progressive about his education, and not one of those parents who censor what their child reads."

It wasn't like she could even stop Wesley from reading whatever book he got his hands on. He'd already read most of the books in the Sheffield Primary School library, and so this year, she started taking him to the local public library.

The woman stood up and looked around her slyly, then reached into her skirt pocket and placed something in

Poppy's hands. "If you find the candidates here lacking, my schedule is open as of the moment. I'm sure we could come to an agreement."

"Excuse me?" Glancing down at her palm, Poppy read the card the young woman had placed in her hand. It read "Allison Brown, Professional Nanny." Then it dawned on her. "Oh, I think there's a misunder—"

"Ms. Baxter? Poppy Baxter?"

At the sound of her name, Poppy shot up from the couch. "Er, that's me."

The woman standing in the doorway peered at her through black-rimmed glasses, though her expression revealed nothing. "Right. Come along this way, please."

"Thank you. One moment if you please." Turning to Wesley, she said, "You have everything you need for now?"

"I'll be fine, Mum." He reached out and put a hand over hers. "You'll get the job. Good luck."

Her heart warmed. Despite how she messed up her own life, she still couldn't believe Wesley had turned out to be such a wonderful child. "Thank you, Wes."

The young woman's expression now turned to disdain as she realized Poppy was not a potential client, but competition. "I'll be taking that, thank you." She snatched the card back and bristled as she turned away and marched back to her seat.

Poppy huffed, then shrugged. *Not like I lied to her.* Turning on her heel, she headed toward the office door, following the woman inside.

"I'm Miriam Fletcher, Director of Placement here at Wilfordshire," she introduced, her voice crisp and clear.

3

"Have a seat, Ms. Baxter." She pointed to the chair in front of the large glass desk, then sat on the seat behind it.

"Thank you." Poppy did as instructed, keeping her back straight as she sat on the edge of the chrome and leather chair.

Ms. Fletcher opened the brown folder sitting on top of her desk, lowering her head as her eyes scanned across the page. "Ms. Baxter. You were a former primary school teacher for six years. So, tell me." She lifted her gaze toward Poppy, eyes boring into her. "Why the sudden career change? Aren't you overqualified to be a nanny?"

Because my wanker of an ex-husband had to get himself involved in a scandal that not only cost him his job, but also mine. Poppy swallowed hard. Though that was the truth, she couldn't say it out loud. But she couldn't lie either, so she settled on the answer she'd practiced at home. "I love—loved my job, truly. The teaching profession is in my blood, and it's always been my dream to mold the fine young minds of the next generation. However, over the years, I felt like I wasn't making much of a difference in the classroom. I wanted to make a more immediate impact by helping parents, by giving them peace of mind knowing their children were safe and happy at home." It wasn't complete rubbish, but she couldn't very well tell Ms. Fletcher that after she was forced to resign from her job, no one else would hire her, and now, nannying was her only choice.

"Ah, I see." Ms. Fletcher closed the folder. "And I assume that the news about your ex-husband's departure from his team has nothing to do with your career change?"

Poppy's stomach sank. *I'm an idiot.*

How could she even think the staff at Wilfordshire

wouldn't look into her background? And it wasn't like it was easy to hide. The press wouldn't leave her and Wesley alone after the news came out about Robbie's true nature. They stalked them everywhere, even at work. But that wasn't even the worst of it. The other teachers and parents were concerned for their safety and those of the other children, and so the headmaster had no choice but ask her to resign *and* ask Wesley to leave the school.

That had been a few weeks ago, before Christmas. She thought the news would die down by now, but it was January, and this was the first callback she'd gotten. She knew the moment anyone saw her name on her CV they'd figure out who she was, so she was surprised to have even gotten this interview in the first place.

"I'm sorry," she murmured as humiliation crept into her chest. Though her knees wobbled, she managed to get up. "I'll see myself out—"

"Wait. Please sit down, Ms. Baxter."

The words stunned her so much that she plopped back into the seat.

"Is it true?" Ms. Fletcher asked. "About your husband?"

"It is." Her lips pursed together. *Fucking Robbie.*

"And your son ..."

The humiliation in her gave way to indignation. "I'm not here to discuss my son," she said in the coldest voice she could muster. "And if you think I'm going to sit here and take your gossip mongering just because I'm desperate for a job, then—"

"Oh no!" Ms. Fletcher interrupted, her face turning a shade of red. "Please. My apologies. I didn't mean for it to come out that way."

"Then why did you call me for an interview if you already knew who I was? And who Robbie is? Am I even here for a real job?"

"You are."

Poppy found herself stunned for a second time. "I-I am?"

She sighed. "Ms. Baxter ... may I call you Poppy?"

She allowed the tension to leave her body. "Yes."

"Then you may call me Miriam." Folding her hands together over the table, she leaned forward. "I can only imagine what you and your son have been going through, and I'm sorry. The holidays must have been difficult."

The woman's change in demeanor and the kindness in her eyes made something break inside Poppy. "I ... yes." She swallowed the tears burning in her throat. *Stupid, stupid Robbie.*

Brash, confident, and arrogant; Robbie Baxter, star of the Wexford Wildebeest rugby club, had been on top of the world. Everyone had celebrated her ex-husband for his natural athletic ability and for leading the team to two consecutive championships. But then one night, a drunken pub fight while out celebrating with his teammates revealed the secret he'd been keeping for years: He was a cheetah shifter. Unfortunately, shifters weren't allowed in human sports leagues because of the unfair advantage of their supernatural speed and strength.

Robbie had been playing professionally for ten years. He'd managed to keep his shifter nature a secret in the smaller leagues and from most people, even Poppy. At nineteen and barely an adult herself when they met, she'd been dazzled by his charm. Then she got pregnant a few months later and they got married. One day, she'd caught him shifting in their backyard, and he confessed everything.

To say that she was shocked was an understatement, and she warned him that he could get caught. She begged him to try another career, but he loved the game so much, and he promised not to use his shifter abilities to gain an unfair advantage or draw any attention.

Of course, that promise barely lasted longer than their marriage.

Five years ago, he'd caught the eye of a Super League scout and was recruited to Wexford. It seemed cliché, but the fame and fortune all went to his head, and he ended up cheating on her multiple times. She stuck around for Wesley's sake, but one day she'd decided enough was enough and filed for divorce.

He kept playing, rose up the ranks, and delivered the championship titles to his team. Only she knew the secret to his success, and after years of waiting for the axe to fall, it was almost a relief when it did. *Almost.*

"Poppy?" Miriam said, interrupting her thoughts. "Are you interested in hearing about this family I'd like to place you with?"

It sounded like there was a catch. But with her savings nearly drained, no job prospects, and on the brink of homelessness, she really didn't have much of a choice. "Yes, please."

"I have one question before we can proceed." Miriam cleared her throat. "You don't have to answer, and if you don't, I won't hold it against you. In fact, if you don't say anything and want to walk out that door, I'll pass your CV along to my colleague at Denham's Staffing, and they've promised to at least call you in for an interview." She took a deep breath. "Your son. He's a shifter?"

Her hands wrung in her lap. "Yes." But that was all she would say about Wesley. She would fight tooth and nail to protect him from those looking to exploit him.

Miriam looked relieved. "Excellent." Reaching into the drawer underneath her desk, she pulled out a sheet of paper and pushed it toward her, along with a pen.

Frowning, she looked at the header on top—Non-Disclosure Agreement.

"It's a standard NDA," Miriam said. "Please take your time reading it and sign only if you agree."

Poppy read the ominous-looking document. A few words that popped out sounded scary to her, like "criminal proceeding" and "legal costs" and "enforceable through courts." She thought about getting up and leaving, but then again, what did she have to lose at this point? Without another thought, she scrawled her name at the bottom.

"Thank you." Miriam put the NDA away and turned back to her. "Now, Poppy. I have a very special, VIP client who's looking for a specific type of nanny. And I believe that with your experience, you're the right candidate."

"M-me?" She blinked. "I'm not sure I understand."

"Well, your son ... he's a shifter, and you raised him, correct?"

She nodded.

"My clients are shifters, and they're looking for someone who could possible stay with them long term. Their child is only a year and half, but I'm told in a year or two, he'll start shifting."

"Ah, right." She remembered those days. Wesley had

been an exceptionally shy child, and his animal had been too. It wasn't really that difficult, rather like having a house cat around. The biggest problem she had was coaxing him down from a tree or finding whatever hidey-hole he was in. After a year or two, he'd outgrown that behavior, and since then, he'd always been in control of his animal, as far as she could tell, and rarely shifted.

"So, you see, they want someone who'll be around for at least two years so the child could get used to their nanny's presence until that time he goes through the change."

"That's fine, but there's something I don't understand," Poppy began. "Why me? I mean, why don't they find a shifter nanny? Surely they have those?"

"Yes, well ..." Miriam sighed. "These shifters are very special. Rather, their animals are. And other shifters aren't comfortable around ... their type." She cleared her throat. "Tell me, Poppy, have you heard of the Northern Isles?"

"Northern Isles?"

"Yes. They're a small kingdom, very reclusive, somewhere in the Norwegian Sea. They're ruled by a special shifter couple."

"Special shifter couple?"

"Yes. The king and queen of the Northern Isles are dragons. As is their son and heir, His Royal Highness, Prince Alric."

"Oh, and—" Poppy's mouth snapped closed as it dawned on her. The *special* clients.

Miriam wanted her to be a nanny to a prince.

A *dragon* prince.

"I ... uh ..." Oh Lord. Her palms started to sweat again. It was one thing to raise a cheetah cub, but another to watch over a *real-life dragon* who could fly and breathe fire. She placed her hands on the table, ready to support herself in case her knees buckled the moment she got up. "I ... thank you for the opportunity but—"

"Please, Poppy!" Miriam got up first. "Will you at least listen to the terms? And allow me to tell you the salary and the benefits?"

Gripping the edge of the table, Poppy managed to nod. "All right."

Miriam told her the amount.

Poppy's jaw nearly unhinged as it dropped. "I beg your pardon?"

The other woman smiled. "You heard me. And that doesn't include your travel, clothing, and food allowance, plus, you'll be provided a private apartment in the palace. There will be bonuses, as well as participation in a pension scheme."

This was a joke, right? But the expression on Miriam's face was entirely serious.

Oh God. With that money, she could do so much for —*Wesley!* "What about my son? I assume they would want me to travel there right away. He ... had to be taken out of school before the holidays, and I haven't made arrangements for him. I suppose my mum and stepdad could look after him." But that would be such an imposition on them as they were now enjoying their retirement years.

"I realized that when I looked into your background," Miriam said. "I've taken the liberty of discussing it with Her Majesty's secretary. She thinks that you're the perfect person for the job, and they'd be willing to accommodate him. Your son can live with you and go to school there. They have an excellent school system in the country and have used English as their standard in the last ten years."

She could keep Wesley with her? And be paid all that money? This was the perfect job. She'd be a fool not to take it.

"Well? What do you think, Poppy?"

She took a long pause. It was a lot of money. More money than she'd ever seen in her entire life. Even when Robbie started playing for Wexford, he'd been stingy with the child maintenance payments. It pained her to see him living the life of a rugby star while she and Wesley had to scrimp and save while living in a shabby two-bedroom flat.

But with what she could earn with this job, by next semester, she'd be able to send Wesley to that private boarding school she knew he'd wanted to attend. But still ... "I'll need to think about it."

"I understand completely," Miriam said. "Do you think you could let me know by the end of the week? I'll be honest with you: I've been doing this for nearly two decades now, and my gut tells me that you're the perfect fit. I mean, you're even half American, correct?"

"Yes, I was born in Boston. My father was a professor in Harvard and met my mother while she was on a work holiday program. We lived in Massachusetts until I was nine. But why does that matter?"

"Her Majesty is American," Miriam said. "Anyway, if you do your research, you'll find out more about Queen Sybil and King Aleksei. I've never met them, but I'm told they're a lovely couple. Now, if you don't mind ..."

"Not at all." Poppy stood up. "I'll let you know by Friday at the latest."

"Excellent. Thank you, Poppy."

"Thank you, Miriam."

It was a miracle she managed to walk out the door as her knees shook with every step. *Dragons!* She knew they existed. She recalled seeing the footage on the news from when that fifty-foot gold dragon stomped around SoHo a few years back. But she'd never actually seen one or been close to one. Robbie was the only shifter she'd ever encountered as even the big shifter groups, especially in England, tended to stay out in the rural areas.

Could she really move to another country and live with them? Work with them? And take care of a dragon prince?

As she left the office, her gaze immediately went to her son. He seemingly hadn't moved an inch the entire time, nose still in his book. *Oh, Wes.* She would do anything to make him happy. He was her life, and she would make the necessary sacrifices to make his dream come true. And she knew this was her chance to give that to him.

And so, two weeks later, that's how Poppy ended up inside the cabin of a plush, private plane, headed to her new home. *The Northern Isles.* Not even saying it in her head or out loud made it real, at least, not until this very moment. Everything had happened so fast, and there was so much to do before their departure—give notice to her landlord, pack up their flat, sell their furniture and store what they could at her mum and stepdad's place.

Then, of course, she had to tell Robbie about the job and that she would be taking Wesley with her. Since she didn't know where he was currently hiding, she had to send him a text so he could sign off on the relocation agreement and visitation revision. He replied he would only sign the papers if she didn't ask for a raise on the maintenance.

The fact that it had been so easy to get him to agree to take their son away shouldn't have surprised Poppy, but it hadn't hurt any less. But she never let it show, nor did she ever speak badly about Robbie in front of Wesley. It was her one rule, and she'd never broken it.

Pushing those thoughts aside, she glanced out the window at the sea underneath them and puffy white clouds flying by.

"Wow, isn't this something?" she said to Wes, who sat across from her. "I didn't think they'd send a whole plane just for us."

Wesley looked up from the personal entertainment system attached to his chair. "There are no commercial flights into the Northern Isles. Of course they would have to send a plane for us."

"Is that so?" she said in a teasing voice. "What else did you learn about the Northern Isles?"

Wes had been surprisingly accepting when she broke the news that she had accepted the job and they would be moving soon. But then again, her son had always been mature and understanding. She would have worried about him missing his friends, but since, well, he had none, it wasn't an issue.

Wesley's brows knitted together. "Not a lot, actually."

"Oh?"

"There wasn't much information," he stated. "Anywhere. I went to the library and asked for books on the Northern Isles, but all they had were some old entries in encyclopedias.

I looked online and didn't see much current news about them."

That was what she'd encountered as well. Miriam had sent her a packet of information about the country, but it was nothing more than a few sheets of paper with dry facts about the capital, main cities, a few useful phrases in the local language, and the weather. Sure, she'd found a few glossy articles and magazine covers from the royal wedding and some local news stories from the queen's hometown, but other than that, there was no news about the country or even current photos of the royal couple in the gossip rags.

"Dragons are secretive, you know," Wes said matter-of-factly. "And very rare. There are only five or six known clans in the world, and no one knows exactly how many there are in existence."

Poppy tensed at the *D* word. Should they be saying that out loud? In here? She wasn't sure, but the idea of seeing a real live dragon set her nerves on edge. *Oh God, this was a mistake.* She shouldn't have agreed to this. Sure, she barely had enough savings to pay for next month's rent, but she could have asked her parents for a loan. Or Robbie.

The thought of crawling to her ex to beg for money made her fear of dragons evaporate. No, she would rather look after a hundred dragon princes than go to him.

"We're nearly there," said the flight steward, Oskar, as he came out of the galley. "I suggest you put your seatbelt on now. Soon after we start to descend, you'll feel the cabin shake and the lights dim for a moment. Don't be alarmed, that's only the magical veil that protects the Northern Isles."

Wesley's eyes widened. "Magical veil? What's it made of? How does it work? Will I be able to see it if I look out?"

Oskar smiled. "I'm afraid I don't know myself, Master Wesley. And no, it is invisible. Now, is there anything else I can get you, Ms. Baxter? Master Wesley?"

"We're fine, thank you, Oskar." Reaching forward, she buckled Wesley's seatbelt, which earned her a pointed look. She smirked at him and shot back with an "I'm-still-your-mum" look. Wesley may be looking forward to going to boarding school in the next semester, but she wasn't. It would be good for him and his future, but she couldn't help feeling sad at the prospect of being separated from him for long periods of time.

Just as Oskar described, the cabin did shake while the lights flickered, but only for a moment. Though her knuckles turned white from gripping her seat's arms, she couldn't help herself and looked out of the window. Clouds blocked her view momentarily as they decreased in altitude, but then the puffy white cottony canopy gave way, revealing a large mass of snow-covered land. First, they flew over what seemed like miles of black sand beach, which then turned to rocky hills, and in the distance, there were snow-capped mountains. Finally, the plane made its final descent into a valley. Poppy supposed in the spring and summer it would be lush and green, but it didn't mean it wasn't beautiful now in the winter. Snow covered most of the land, and a few trees were left bare, but there was a stillness about it that appealed to her.

"Welcome to the Northern Isles," Oskar greeted as he re-entered the cabin once the plane stopped.

We're really here. Excitement, fear, and a rush of something she couldn't name all mixed up in her belly.

After getting up from their seats and gathering their

carry-on luggage, Oskar led them out of the plane. She shivered as the frigid air hit her, and beside her, Wesley tugged on his jacket tighter.

At the foot of the steps was a figure wrapped up in a thick wool coat. She held out her hand once Poppy reached the bottom of the staircase. "Poppy, it's nice to meet you in person. I'm so glad you could push your departure forward a week. Oh, and welcome to the Northern Isles."

Poppy immediately recognized the blonde, middle-aged woman with the bright smile from their previous video chats—Melina Gunnarson, secretary to Her Majesty, Queen Sybil. "Likewise, Melina." She took the offered hand and shook it. "And this is my son, Wesley."

"Hello, Wesley," Melina greeted and offered her hand as well, which Wesley shook. "I hope you both had a good trip. I see you were warmly welcomed by our famous winters," she chuckled. "Now, let's head into the car before we all freeze."

They hurried into the black SUV waiting on the tarmac, with Melina slipping into the front seat while she and Wesley piled into the back.

"Another car will take your things to the palace and your apartments," she explained. "It's about a forty-five-minute drive to Helgeskar Palace in the capital city, Odelia. If you are tired, please feel free to nap, or if not, ask me any questions."

"I think I'm too wired to nap," she joked. "The jet was lovely and so comfortable. Oskar was most accommodating, and the food, too, was excellent." It was better than any fancy restaurant at London—not that she ate at those frequently. "Please thank Her Majesty for Wesley and me."

"You may tell her yourself. You're both to meet her for lunch at her glasshouse in the royal gardens when we arrive."

"Oh my." A private lunch with the queen? "Is that ... normal for a royal?" She doubted the queen of England ever met with her children's nannies.

There was a twinkle in the other woman's eyes. "I think you'll find that there are few things about Her Majesty that are 'normal' for a royal."

Well, there was the part where she turned into a giant, fire-breathing dragon, but Poppy did her best to quash the anxiety building in her. Looking over at Wesley as he peered out the window with his nose pressed up to the glass, she reminded her herself why she was doing this.

I need this job. Her initial contract would have her working here for three months on probation, and after that, the queen would decide on whether to renew her contract for another two years and every two years after that. Everything hinged on her performance over the coming weeks, and she vowed to do her best so she could stay on for at least until Wesley finished boarding school. That was the goal, and she would devote her energy to that for the next few years.

Settling back into her seat, Poppy, too, decided to look out at the scenery. As they pulled onto the highway, there was nothing but evergreen trees and snow-covered ground outside, and the occasional patch of clearing or an odd farmhouse or two. About thirty minutes later, the rural scenery gradually made way for an urban landscape, which became even more modern as they turned onto an exit with signage that indicated this was the way to Odelia.

"It's a beautiful city," she declared as they entered what looked like the main city center. The small stone buildings and cobbled streets had that European charm, but the streets were paved and modern vehicles filled them.

"Many of the structures are original, and if we have to build new ones, they must be kept in the old style," Melina explained. "But I assure you, we're very modern here. We use one hundred percent renewable energy, and all vehicles are electric."

"That's brilliant," Wesley piped up. "How did they manage that?"

"We've always had to fend for ourselves being an archipelago," she said. "It was mostly out of necessity. Our royal family does try to preserve the old ways and culture, though we're trying to adapt to the outside world as well. For example, our previous monarch, King Harald, declared English as an official language over a decade ago. You'll find many of the younger people speak it, and the school you'll be in will have classes in both English and Nordgensprak."

"Could I learn it?" Wesley asked. "Nordgensprak, I mean. I tried to search for books or apps that could teach me, but I couldn't find any."

"If you wish," Melina said. "You're already enrolled and set to start school in a week, but your mother will be meeting with your teacher before then." She looked to Poppy. "There are some files and a laptop in your apartment that has all the information, including how to set up an appointment with Wesley's homeroom teacher."

"That's wonderful." She smiled over at Wesley, who beamed at her. He reminded her so much of his namesake, her deceased father. The elder Wesley loved books and reading too.

"Until then—oh, we're nearly there." Melina nodded toward the outside.

As the SUV approached the large, imposing castle up ahead, Poppy couldn't stop herself from gasping. "That's—"

"Helgeskar Castle," Wesley said, his mouth agape. "It's humongous."

"The castle occupies twelve acres, has fifteen main buildings, eight hundred rooms and one hundred fireplaces," Melina rattled.

"That's almost as big as Windsor Castle," he stated. "Windsor has three hundred fireplaces."

Melina chuckled. "Ah, yes. Well, our kings are dragons after all and have no need for so much heat, even in the winter."

Wesley's brows furrowed. "The dragons here … they're water dragons, right?"

"Wesley," Poppy admonished. Oh God, could they say things like that here? "I'm sorry, you don't have to answer that."

"Oh, it's quite all right," Melina assured her. "I know our royal family can be secretive, but seeing as you'll be working closely with them, it's good to know these things. And, Wesley, you promise not to tell anyone outside the Northern Isles about what you see here, correct?"

His head bobbed up and down. "Yes, I promise."

"Good. And yes, you're correct. The dragons of the Northern Isles are water dragons."

"So, they don't breathe fire?"

Poppy felt relief wash over her. *Maybe I should have done more research about dragons.* Or asked Wesley.

"No, they do not, but they can breathe underwater, fly,

and swim long distances. But Queen Sybil, who you'll meet shortly, is a mountain dragon. She's the one who breathes fire. In fact, that's one of her titles. The Great Fire Breather."

And her stomach tied itself in knots again.

"Well, here we are." The SUV slowed to a stop inside a large courtyard. "I do apologize for not giving you time to get settled in, but Her Majesty is very busy, and this is the only time this week she'll be able to meet you."

"That's perfectly all right." In fact, Poppy was glad to have it over with sooner than later. "And you, Wesley, are you feeling all right? Not too tired?"

"I'm fine, Mum. I want to meet the dragon queen." He sounded almost excited at the prospect.

Melina smiled brightly. "Excellent. Come along then, we shouldn't keep her waiting."

They got out of the vehicle and followed her through an archway, which led out into a spacious garden surrounded by tall, black stone walls. Most of the trees and shrubs were bare, but she could imagine how gorgeous it would be in full bloom.

Melina motioned for them to turn down a long path that led up to a stunning glasshouse in the middle of the garden.

"Hold onto me, Wes." She grabbed Wesley's hands. "You don't have proper boots on; you might slip and fall."

"Wow!" Wesley exclaimed, his eyes wide as he soaked in the sight of the beautiful white structure. "Are there tropical plants in there? Or palm trees?"

"Why, yes," Melina said. "Our orchids bloom year round."

"I want to see!" Wesley broke free of Poppy's grip and dashed down the snowy path toward the conservatory.

"Wes!" she warned. "Be careful!" Still, she couldn't bear to chasten him anymore as this was the most she'd seen him excited about anything.

"While the castle dates back to—"

A large, piercing screech interrupted Melina, and a large shadow loomed overhead. "What the—" Poppy gasped as she lifted her gaze to the sky. A gigantic, snake-like creature was flying overhead. It was probably fifty feet long and covered from head to tail in blue scales and translucent wings that fanned out.

A dragon.

And it was heading straight for Wesley.

Poppy watched in horror as the dragon made a wide U-turn and began to descend, then its body stretched out straight as a missile, honing in on its target at breakneck speed.

"No!" Poppy cried as adrenaline pumped through her veins and pushed her to sprint down the path toward her son. Melina shouted something at her, but she didn't pay it any mind as her focus was on Wesley.

He stood, frozen to the spot, head lifted up as the dragon came closer. "Run, Wes!" she cried.

He must have heard her because he turned toward her. "Mum!"

From then on, everything happened so fast. One moment he was running down the path as she met him halfway, and the next, a small, furry bundle leapt into her arms as Wesley's clothes lay in a heap on the snowy dirt path.

Twisting her body around, she cradled the cub in her arms, shielding it from the threat. It didn't matter that her enemy was a giant monster that could probably gobble her up whole. No, she was protecting her son, and she would die before she let anything harm him.

And so, she braced herself, waiting for something to happen. Her body tensed as she held her breath and closed her eyes. There was a loud *whoosh*, and a strong wind nearly knocked her over. An eternity seemed to pass before she finally found the courage to turn and lift her head.

The dragon was gone. However, a towering figure stood inches away, looming over them. But he wasn't just tall; he was enormous. Possibly the biggest man she'd ever seen at nearly seven feet tall, plus he was built like a wall. His powerful legs were encased in tight-fitting brown leather pants. The loose, white linen shirt he wore spanned across a wide chest, the deep V in the middle exposing a tantalizing amount of tanned skin and a curl of ink peeked from the edge of the fabric.

Setting her gaze higher, she stared up at his face. Most of it was covered with a reddish beard that matched his hair, but it didn't hide the intensity of his bright green eyes. Eyes that bore into her very soul and made her heart stop for a moment before it once again thudded like a drum, beating against her rib cage.

Seeing as the dragon disappeared and this man appeared out of nowhere, Poppy could venture an educated guess as to what happened.

It looked like she'd finally met a real-life dragon.

CHAPTER 2

Rorik's day had started out like any other. He woke up before the sun rose as he did every day since he was but a mere child of seven. After gearing up, he went for a brisk, one-hour jog around the grounds, then a one-hour swim in the sea in dragon form before heading back to the palace. And as usual, he had barely gotten through the door of his office when the demands of his position as captain of the Dragon Guard hurtled at him like darts.

Three people were already waiting outside his office, and he hadn't even had breakfast. Once he'd finished those meetings, there were other matters to attend to. There was the weekly roster to arrange, training sessions to schedule, intelligence reports to read, security meetings with various palace staff, and complaints to field.

At first, he had thought the promotion was an honor. His father, Neils, had been captain for the current king's grandfather before he retired, and so was his father before him. In fact, his family, the House of Asulf, produced many fine dragon guards and captains in the last three hundred years.

But with all the responsibilities on his shoulders—responsibilities that took him away from actual training and guard duties—the leadership position seemed more like a curse.

As if he wasn't already busy with his duties, just recently, his king and queen tasked him with finding a long-lost prince who'd been missing for decades.

What else could possibly try to shove itself onto my already full plate?

Well, perhaps he should not have asked.

Mine.

His dragon's deep roar sent a shock wave through him, making it difficult to move. Or breathe. Or speak. He could only stare down at the small, but magnificent woman in front of him.

His fingers itched to reach out and touch her smooth, sepia skin and brush the disarray of dark springy coils of hair away from her delicate, heart-shaped face. Eyes the color of obsidian opened wide as her lush lips parted.

Mine, came the call again.

The truth came from his very bones: this beautiful female was his fated mate.

"What the bloody hell were you thinking?" she roared. "You could have hurt him!"

"E-excuse me, my lady?" He blinked. "Hurt who?"

"My son!"

"Your son?" Searching around, he could not find anyone else present. "Where—" His gaze lowered. "What in Odin's beard is that?" There was a tiny, spotted bundle curled up in her arms.

"*That* is my son," she said through gritted teeth. With a

deep sigh, she began to stroke the creature's furry body. "There, there, Wes. It's all right. Mum's here."

"What's going on here? I heard a—Rorik?"

Rorik stiffened at the sound of his queen's voice. "Your Majesty." He turned in her direction and bowed deep.

Queen Sybil of the Northern Isles narrowed her eyes at him. *What are you doing here? Did you fly in,* she asked through their mental link. Though she was not a water dragon like him and the rest of the Dragon Guard, as the fated and bonded mate to his king, she could speak to him without words.

I can explain, My Queen, he answered. *I was—*

"Poppy, I—" Melina Gunnarson came running toward them and stopped short when she saw the queen. "Your Majesty." She made a deep curtsey.

"Your—oh!" The mystery woman—his *mate*—sputtered something incoherent, and then curtseyed as well. Her son—a cheetah cub, from the looks of it—peered up from the shelter of her arms and blinked at the queen.

Queen Sybil placed her hands on her hips. "Can someone tell me what's going on?"

"Your Majesty, this is Poppy Baxter," Melina began. "And her son. Wesley."

The queen's face brightened. "Lovely to meet you, Poppy." Her mouth tugged at the corners. "And you too, Wesley," she said, nodding at the cub. Frowning, she turned to Rorik. "I was waiting inside the glasshouse—did I hear your dragon screeching like a banshee? And swooping down to attack?"

"He scared my son," the woman—Poppy—said. She kept her eyes lowered, but continued. "Wesley just got a little excited and started running toward the glasshouse." Raising her head, she sent him a seething look. "Then this ... *oaf* comes flying in, claws and teeth out, ready to attack my son."

"What?" Queen Sybil exclaimed. *Rorik, is this true?* "Is that true?" she repeated out loud.

"I can explain, Your Majesty." The words barely made it out of his mouth as his chest squeezed tight. His mate, the one that fate decreed was the other half of his soul, stared at him with contempt. It was too much. Not to mention, his dragon scurried about in confusion. It could not understand why their mate seemed to despise them. No, it wanted him to claim her now. But how?

Ahem. The queen raised a brow at him.

"Uh, yes." But how was he to explain how he'd arrived at this moment in the first place? "Your Majesty, while checking your schedule today, I saw that you had planned a private lunch in the gardens with two foreign guests. When neither Gideon nor Niklas could tell me who these guests were nor had any files on them been passed onto my office for review, I decided to investigate myself." Her safety, after all, was of utmost importance. If anything were to happen to Queen Sybil, it would be on his head, and King Aleksei would never forgive him. "I was only protecting you, Your Majesty."

"By scaring a little boy?" his mate interjected.

Each word stung at his heart, but he swallowed it down. "I only saw a blur and felt the presence of an unknown shifter making his way towards Her Majesty." As he flew toward the gardens, he's spied the fast-moving blur darting toward the glasshouse. "And I had no idea it was just the boy. As I mentioned, I was not informed that we had unvetted individuals coming into the palace grounds." Even though they were in the Northern Isles and within Helgeskar Palace, that didn't mean they could be lax in security. Their enemies were still out there, after all, and two years ago, they had nearly succeeded in their plan of infiltrating the country.

"Ms. Baxter's file has been on your desk for a week, Rorik," Melina said, her tone clipped.

Damn paperwork. He was raised to be a dragon guard. A warrior. Not a pencil pusher. If he had known that there was so much paperwork to be done, he would have spent hours on his computer skills instead of learning how to disarm an enemy. Why did his father never tell him about this part of the job? Neils should have sent him to secretarial school during the summers, instead of those intense training camps in the Rejykjarholl mountains.

The queen cleared her throat. "Poppy Baxter is Alric's new nanny. And Rorik is captain of the Dragon Guards," she explained. "Which means he's in charge of security for the royal family and the entire palace."

His dragon urged him to make things right. "I apologize, my lady," he said, bowing his head. "For scaring you and your cub."

"Captain …" His mate inhaled a quick breath. "I … uh, I didn't realize that you … you were only doing your job." Her arms held the cub tighter. "I should have kept an eye on him. I'm sorry for shouting at you."

"I decided on the switch in schedule at the last minute when I realized I would only have time to meet Poppy today," the queen said. "The schedule change must not have reached your office in time."

"Clearly a misunderstanding." Melina clapped her hands together. "And now that we are all acquainted, perhaps we should head in to lunch? Her Majesty has a meeting with the dean of the university at half past one."

"Yes," the queen agreed. "Let's head to the glasshouse, shall we? And thank you, Rorik. I'll see you later." *Good save with the apology, by the way*, she added cheekily as she led them away. *I think she appreciated it.*

Of course, My Queen. He would apologize to his mate a thousand times if it meant she would never look at him with loathing again.

Oh, Yggdrasil.

His mate. Poppy Baxter. And she had a son. Was there a rival male in the picture? The cub's father had to be a shifter as he could tell Poppy was human.

An ugly, unnamed feeling crept into his stomach, curling up like a snake making its home in a pit.

Where was this male? Was he still in their lives? What cad would let his cub and woman fly alone to an unknown country by themselves?

The questions swirled around in his brain, and the snake churned up a bitter storm in his stomach. Before he knew it, he was making his way toward the glasshouse.

Wait.

This was utter ridiculousness.

But his dragon would not listen and urged him on, stirring the feelings he now recognized as jealousy inside him. It had to know if another had claimed their mate.

Despite himself, Rorik continued and Cloaked himself, his body turning invisible so no one could detect him as he slipped into the conservatory. Years of training had also taught him how to remain stealthy and silent. The queen was a shifter herself and would be able to detect his presence through sound. He blocked their mental link, too, just in case.

He crept deeper inside, past the exotic ferns and orchid blooms, and the artificial ponds and waterfalls of the hothouse garden. Making his way to the center court where he knew the queen would have her luncheon set up, he stopped a few feet away, staking a spot behind a sizable tropical plant, and peered from behind its wide leaves. From here, he could see Queen Sybil at the head of the dining table, her back to him, Melina on her left, and Poppy on her right. Sitting beside her was a young boy.

"... and did you enjoy the trip over here, Wesley?" Queen Sybil asked.

"I did, Your Majesty." His head bobbed up and down vigorously. "You have a nice jet."

"Thank you, and I'm glad to hear that you had a good trip. I hope you'll like going to King Hakkonnen Elementary. It's a great school, though I've only visited a few times. But what are you going to do while you wait for classes to begin on Monday?"

The boy paused. "Well, I suppose I could read some of my favorite books again. Mum made me leave most of them at Grandma and Grandpa's but I brought along the ones I really, really need. I've read them many times, but I still like them."

"Books, huh? Wow, I didn't think kids your age still read them."

"You know, Wesley," Melina interjected. "There is a library in the palace."

"Really?"

"Oh, yeah," the queen exclaimed. "Please feel free to go

in and hang out. And you can borrow as many books as you want."

"I can?"

"Of course. I'm the queen, and I say you can."

"Brilliant!" Wesley clapped his hands together. "I can't take out more than three books at our library."

"Y-Your Majesty, you are too generous," Poppy stammered.

"It's no trouble at all. And I'm so happy you decided to accept the job, Poppy."

"Thank you, Your Majesty. I really am grateful for this opportunity. And thank you for allowing me to bring Wesley and have him go to school here."

"Of course, I wouldn't dream of separating you from him. We have more than enough room. I'm just glad his father allowed him to go."

Rorik couldn't see what happened but heard the sound of a glass tumbling over.

"Oh no!"

"Mum!" Wesley admonished.

Poppy sounded like she'd choked on something. "Oh, bug —uh... apologies, Your Majesty. Sorry, Wes. Didn't mean to spill my drink all over you."

"No worries. It's just orange juice." Queen Sybil turned to Melina. "Would you mind escorting Wesley to the bathrooms and helping him get cleaned up?"

"No! He's my son, I should—"

"I don't mind at all." Melina got up and circled around to where the boy sat. "Here we go, Wesley. Let's wash off that stain before it settles in then." She helped him out of his chair and led him away.

"I-I'm sorry," Poppy said, her voice shaking.

"It's all right, Poppy." Queen Sybil assured her. "And I apologize for bringing your ex-husband up in the conversation."

Ex-husband. So, she was divorced. Relief poured through him knowing she was not bound to her son's father. Now that his dragon had its answer, he knew it was time to go. And he *was* about to leave, but curiosity got the best of him, especially when he heard her next words.

"You know all about it then. About Robbie and the scandal."

Scandal?

"I mean, of course you do," Poppy continued glumly. "Your team must have looked into my background and records since birth. You probably even know about that time I got called to the principal's office for punching James Darden during recess in first grade."

"I'm sure he deserved it," Queen Sybil chuckled. "But, yes. I know about what your ex-husband did." The queen snorted. "Hiding his shifter nature was one thing, but then playing in the human rugby leagues when it wasn't allowed is another. There's a reason humans are so prejudiced against us, and it really takes just one bad apple to rot the entire barrel. And the blowback on you and Wes." She tsked. "It must have been difficult. I've had to deal with the press myself in the last two years. *And* you got fired from your job too."

Rorik tightened his hands into fists. *What a cad.*

"It was difficult." Poppy sighed. "I really am grateful for this job. But if I may ask a question ..." She took a pause. "Miriam said that you wanted someone who knew how to be around a shifter child, and I understand that. But with the scandal and Robbie's deception ... why choose me? Shouldn't you choose someone with a spotless record? Who won't bring scandal to your country?"

The queen leaned forward, and Rorik guessed she must have taken Poppy's hand. "First of all, that 'scandal' you're talking about wasn't on you. It was all your ex's fault. Second, I looked at *your* records. Your accomplishments, in particular—top grades in your GCSEs, high marks in all your undergraduate courses, and glowing recommendations from your professors. And you were pregnant with Wesley in your final year, I'm guessing?"

She nodded.

"You've been a primary school teacher for the last seven years and were well-loved by your students. The administration was forced to fire you because of what happened with your ex, and they made you take Wesley out of school too."

"Th-they thought he might be a danger to the other students. That he didn't have any control—oh, but he does! I swear, he's a good kid."

Rorik gnashed his teeth. Those humans thought that tiny little creature was a danger? What kind of ignorant, idiotic fools were they?

"I know," Queen Sybil soothed. "But to answer your question: Have you ever been faced with a decision and you immediately listened to your gut? Like, really listened to it, and despite whatever everyone else said, you just went with it?"

Poppy paused before answering as she turned her head in the direction of the path to the bathrooms. Melina and

Wesley walked toward them, his shirt clean of the orange stain. "Yes." Her lips slowly curved into a smile. "One time."

"And there you go. When I saw your application, I had a feeling that there was something special about you. And now I know I made the right decision." The queen sounded giddy. "Your experience with a shifter child was a big factor, but I'm sure I could have easily found someone with the same qualifications. Raising dragon children isn't easy—just ask my mother, she had three of us." She chuckled. "But I wanted someone who had the right *instincts*. And I can tell you have them."

"I ... thank you, Your M-Majesty," she stammered. "I can only hope I don't disappoint you."

Rorik's dragon snorted, as if it doubted she could do that. She was their mate. Of course she had the skill and instincts to raise dragon children.

However, another feeling crept into his gut. Before he could act on it or be discovered, he crept away from the courtyard and headed toward the exit.

Coming out from the hot, humid atmosphere of the glasshouse, the frigid air outside stung him like a slap to the face. His shifter body immediately adjusted, but the change in temperature was enough to cool the burning he was feeling.

The information he had gleaned could easily be confirmed by reading the files sitting on his desk, so he quickly shifted and flew up into the cool gray winter skies. With practiced ease, he slid between skins, landing on the balcony outside his office in his human form with a soft thud. Striding inside, he rifled through the piles of folders on his desk, found the right one, sat down, and read through the file silently.

It was true. All of it. Rorik could feel the anger welling up inside him. At her ex-husband's deception. And the fallout Poppy and her son had endured. And then being fired from a career she obviously loved and having to take the job as a nanny overseas.

What an injustice. Paper and cardboard wrinkled in his hands as his fingers curled around the folder. How he wished he could go after everyone who had hurt her. The administrators at her former job. The paparazzi who had camped in front of their home and gossip rags that called them all sorts of vile names. And her fool of an ex-husband. They would all pay. His dragon nodded in agreement.

But another thought popped into his head. The rational human part of him. She was a virtual stranger and new to the Northern Isles. And obviously, human, meaning she did not know anything about being mates. How was he going to explain it to her? Let her know about their connection? And how would he initiate the mating bond so he could claim her and be with her forever?

A knock on the door jolted him out of his reverie. "Come in!" he said rather grouchily.

"Captain?" A head popped in through the doorway. It was Gillard, the royal steward. "I'm here for our meeting regarding the security for this Friday's state dinner."

He groaned inwardly. How he wished he could go out into the training fields and practice with his sword. Surely his skills had dulled by now. *But duty calls.* "Come in, Gillard. Let's get started." That way, they could get this over with sooner.

Rorik's duties had occupied him for the rest of the day and the evening as well, which proved a good distraction. His dragon, though, did not appreciate being ignored and put aside. It longed for their mate. To hear her voice or maybe even see her smile. But as captain of the Dragon Guard, he had to put duty above everything else.

The following day, however, the dragon continued to let its displeasure be known. Rorik could barely contain it and nearly scared the kitchen staffer who had brought in his lunch. Shoving away from his desk, he made a decision and canceled all his meetings, dressed in his armor, then stalked out of his office.

With purposeful strides, he marched out of the palace through the rear courtyard and made his way to the training grounds across the lawn where the sounds of clashing metal, heavy grunts, and cheers greeted him.

He'd never felt more at home.

The sounds, the smells, and the electricity crackling in the air reminded him of his childhood. Being born into the House of Asulf, the greatest warrior family in the Northern Isles, Rorik knew he would someday be part of the Dragon Guard. Indeed, he'd trained for it all his life, and it was the biggest honor of his life when, at the age of seventeen, he'd been the youngest dragon ever chosen for such an honor.

The king's ward, Thoralf, had just been chosen as captain the year before Rorik joined, so he knew he might not have the chance to be captain, but Neils had been proud of him just the same. When Thoralf left two years ago to go on his quest, he had chosen Rorik to succeed him. *You will do well, my friend,* Thoralf had said. *But I should warn you: There's more to this job than you might think.*

Initially, Rorik had scoffed at Thoralf's warning. He was of the House of Asulf, built from dragon warrior stock. Being captain was in his blood, and Rorik had been confident it would not be much harder than his normal duties.

Now he had come to eat his own words. *You were right, my friend.*

As he drew closer to his destination, the sounds grew even louder. When he came upon the combat ring—which was a fenced-off area in the middle of the training grounds, he observed the two fighters inside as they charged at each other, one holding a sword and the other, a large axe.

Of course, such weapons were not only archaic, but also unnecessary as they were, after all, dragon shifters and could easily take down a foe with their claws and teeth. But, training with weapons was a tradition, dating back hundreds of years to when their kind first landed on the Northern Isles.

When he was a child, he had questioned his father why they had to train with swords and shields or even learn hand-to-hand combat when they had modern weapons. Neils had explained that, "It's not just tradition, but learning to fight also teaches you discipline and resourcefulness. There may come a time where you might be unable to call upon your dragon, so you must learn how to defend yourself by any means necessary."

Rorik shivered at that last thought. He never would have believed that it was possible to lose one's dragon, but then he'd seen it happen two years ago with his own eyes.

"Enough!" came the gravelly, rough roar from Stein,

current weapons master of the Dragon Guards. "I said, enough!"

The two combatants stepped apart. "I almost had him," spat the one with the sword.

"You had nothing, Magnus," the axe-wielder shot back.

Stein grit his teeth, his heavy, midnight black braid swinging as he marched toward them. "This is an exercise. You're not meant to kill each other today."

"I thought Dragon Guards were supposed to be strong? And fierce?" Magnus asked. "Isn't that why we're training? So we can protect our king?"

"Yes, a Dragon Guard must be strong," Stein began. "However, he must also learn discipline and how to fight intelligently, without anger or fear clouding his mind. Or *personal* matters." He narrowed his gaze at both of therm. "And you are still both prospects. Neither of you, or any of you"—he turned sharply to the three other men on the sidelines—"are Dragon Guards yet."

Being part of the Dragon Guard was not a duty to be taken lightly. They were tasked with the protection of the very heart and soul of the Northern Isles—the king and his family. Two years ago, their enemies, the Knights of Aristaeum, attacked the country and did the unthinkable—used a magical artifact called The Wand of Aristaeum to take away the previous king's dragon. Without his animal, the then-King Harald had to abdicate, and his son Prince Aleksei had to step up as king. It had brought shame to Thoralf, which was why he had left in the first place and Rorik had been promoted, albeit temporarily, until Thoralf returned with the cure to restore the former king's dragon.

Rorik had been torn at the thought of training a new

batch of prospects. On one hand, they badly needed the help. With the queen and now the crown prince, they were stretched thin. But bringing a new Dragon Guard into the fold was akin to accepting that Thoralf's departure was permanent.

Thoralf will succeed, and he will find a cure, he said to himself. Putting those negative thoughts away, he trudged into the combat ring.

"Captain!" One of the recruits spied him and his entire body tensed. The rest fell into line, their backs ramrod straight and gazes locked ahead into the distance.

Stein turned around. *There is no inspection scheduled today. What are you doing here?*

Blunt and direct as always. *I'm not here for an inspection, Stein. I just ... got bored being inside all day.* Stein preferred to speak through their mental link, especially with other people around.

The other dragon snorted. *Come to see this sorry lot then?*

I can see your standards are as unreachable as always. Stein was one of the fiercest men he knew, and his skill in combat both in and out of dragon form was what made him a good weapons master. *So, not one of these men, who are supposed to be the cream of the crop of the Dragon Navy, are up to the task?*

Maybe those last two fools. His eyes tracked to the two combatants. *Magnus and Ranulf are at the top of the dungheap. But then again, so are flies.*

It really was a shame Stein didn't speak out loud so much. He was a veritable poet with insults. "You two," he called to the men. "What houses are you from?"

The younger of the two spoke first. "Magnus of House

Asgeir."

"Ranulf of House Dalgaard," axe-wielder said.

No wonder they seemed eager to tear each other's throats. Asgeir and Dalgaard had a long-standing feud dating back many generations. In fact, it had gone on so long, Rorik was pretty sure neither side could remember how it started.

"At ease." He studied the two men. The way they were complete opposites was almost comical. Handsome, tall, and slender, Magnus's blue eyes glowed bright like sapphires, and his golden hair gleamed in the sun. Ranulf, on the other hand, had no hair on his tattoo-covered head. The ink extended down his neck and past his brawny shoulders. The thick beard that covered half his face only made him look fiercer.

"Excellent fighting form," he began. "But I agree with Stein." Both men were from loyal dragon families, though if they were recruited from the Dragon Navy, that meant they were from a lower branch of their houses. "Perhaps you need—"

Well, what do we have here? Came a familiar voice through their mental link.

"His Majesty, the king!" Stein called out.

All five recruits immediately bent down on one knee, and Stein and Rorik spun around to face King Aleksei, bowing deeply.

"You may rise," King Aleksei ordered.

As Rorik lifted his head, his heart slammed against his rib cage when he realized the king was not alone. He carried his young son, Crown Prince Alric, in his arms, and coming up behind him was—

Mine!

The sight of his mate sent a shock wave through him. And when he saw her heaving and struggling to push the prince's pram through the grass and dirt, he immediately rushed to her side.

"Allow me," he said.

Her shoulders tensed, then her head lifted up. Dark eyes—oh, he could lose himself in them for days—widened for a moment, the pupils dilating. Then she frowned and huffed. "N-no, thank you, Captain Rorik."

No one called him that, but he would correct her later. Right now, he needed to help, so he drew closer, reaching out to take the handles from her. "That pram was not made for such terrain as this. Please allow me—"

She gritted her teeth. "I said, no thank you. I can manage it."

His dragon roared at him to help her anyway. "It would be easier for—"

"Rorik? Poppy? What's going on here?"

He turned his head and saw King Aleksei had come up to them. "Your Majesty. I was offering Ms. Baxter my assistance as she's having trouble with the prince's baby carriage."

"I w-was *not*," she sputtered. "Will you please just let me do my job?"

There it was again. The disdain in her voice and the look of contempt on her face. His stomach tied up in knots. He took a few steps back and raised his hands in surrender. "Of course. My apologies."

King Aleksei raised a brow at him. *Is everything all right?*

Yes, My King. He cleared his throat. "I should attend to my duties. Good day, Ms. Baxter. Your Majesty." Turning on his heel, he stalked away.

Rorik? came the king's voice in his head. *What's wrong?*

I have matters to attend to, Your Majesty. Not wanting to discuss it further, he shut the mental link between them.

He was sorely tempted to shift into his dragon form, but knowing his beast, it just might turn around and go back to her. *No,* he warned his dragon, even as it lifted its head to agree with that idea. *We have obviously done something to offend her.* But what, he didn't know.

Oh, Yggdrasil. He scrubbed a hand down his face. He'd been trained in weapons and combat. How to fight. How to be a warrior. How to defend his king and country. Women, too, he knew plenty about as he never lacked of female company when he felt the urge. But what he knew about mates wouldn't even be enough to fill a thimble.

Didn't the gods or fate or some higher power deem her to be his? For their souls to be entwined? Did she not feel the powerful pull of the urge to bond as he did? Why did she act like he was some odorous being?

Perhaps his animal was wrong. Maybe she wasn't his mate, and it somehow had its signals crossed.

His dragon shook its head vehemently. *Mine.*

Well then, if you're so sure, tell me what in Frigga's name must I to do to win her over?

But the dragon could only heave one long, sad sigh.

Yes, that's what I thought.

As Rorik crossed the threshold back into the castle, the thoughts of his mate's disdain plagued him, but he could not find any explanation or answer. He headed straight to his office, and for once, he was glad for the duties that would distract him for the time being.

CHAPTER 3

Poppy stared after the captain of the guard's retreating back, the oxygen finally making its way back into her lungs. She initially thought that jet lag, excitement, or perhaps just something in the air in the Northern Isles made her react that way to Captain Rorik's towering presence during their first meeting yesterday.

But no, the moment she looked up into those eyes, she'd felt it again—a powerful pull that made it difficult to ignore him, and a low, simmering heat in her belly that built up the longer she was around him.

Oh, dear God, no.

She couldn't be attracted to him. She *can't*. Well, obviously, she could, but who wouldn't be? The captain of the Dragon Guard was entirely too tempting for his own good. Ginger men weren't usually her type as she normally went for dark and handsome, like Robbie. But on Captain Rorik, there was something appealing about it and made her want to rake her fingers through the wild red locks.

And his clothes—or rather, lack of clothes—just about

sent her temperature into the stratosphere. He wore the same leather pants as yesterday, but no shirt. Instead, gold armor covered his muscled arms, and a leather strap was slung across his wide chest. There was that bit of ink teasing her again under the gold buckle, but she quickly averted her gaze before she could make out what it was.

Her hands had hung onto the pram for dear life, her knees wobbling as she could practically feel the heat of his body as he stood inches away from her. God, she wondered what it would be like to press herself up—

"Poppy?"

The king's voice jolted her out of her lust-fueled thoughts. "What? Oh—I mean, yes, Your Majesty?" Feeling like an idiot, she felt the blush creep up her neck.

King Aleksei's assessing gaze bore into her. "Are you all right?"

"I am, Your Majesty." She nodded at Prince Alric. "Uh, shall I take His Highness and put him back in the pram?"

"No, no. I quite enjoy carrying him around." His handsome face lit up as he bounced the adorable little boy up and down. Alric giggled and grabbed a fistful of his father's hair.

No one had been more surprised than Poppy when the king himself showed up in the nursery that morning. Though they'd been formally introduced the previous night, she didn't expect to see him quite so soon.

There was something about being in the presence of the dragon king that was overwhelming. Not like the way she felt around the captain, but even as a human, she could tell there was something different about King Aleksei, a power and confidence that had everyone paying attention, and not just because he was a monarch. When he strode in so casually into the nursery, she'd dropped Alric's bottle. Apparently, his morning meeting with a minister had been canceled, and so he wanted to take the prince on a walk and asked her to accompany them.

She couldn't say no; he was the king, after all. Still, she'd been on tenterhooks the entire time. Would he go into an all-out inquisition? Did he approve of his wife's choice of nanny for the crown prince? She was a bundle of nerves the entire walk here.

Of course, running into the much too attractive captain of the guard hadn't helped. She hadn't meant to be so standoffish around him, but King Aleksei was there. No one wanted to look incompetent around their employer, so she brushed him away, even if he insisted on helping her.

"Looks like training is over for the day." The king nodded toward the group of men inside what appeared to be a paddock in the middle of the field. "I was hoping Alric would be able to watch them, but we are too late." Turning to them, he lifted a hand. "Carry on!" When the men scurried about, he said to her, "Let's head back, shall we?"

"Yes, Your Majesty." She attempted to turn the pram around, but the wheels were now fully mired in the mud. *Oh dear.* "If you give me a moment—oh!"

The king reached over and grabbed one of the handles and lifted it with one hand, then turned it around. "It should be easier this time as it's downhill. I shouldn't have asked you to push it all the way up here." He frowned. "Perhaps you should take Alric and I shall push?"

"No, it's all right, Your Majesty. As you said, it should be easier from here." Her heart warmed at the sight of the smiling baby boy, obviously thrilled being in his father's arms.

"Besides, you should enjoy every minute you can of being able to carry him like that. One day, you're going to put him down and never pick him back up again."

He looked at Alric, a fond smile on his face. "You are very wise, Poppy. I can see why my wife chose you."

The compliment made her blush. "Thank you, Your Majesty."

"Not that I do not trust her judgement. I can see you are very capable, and your background is most impressive. Isn't being a nanny a step down from your previous position as a teacher?"

"Childcare is not a lowly job." The words sounded harsh, so she added, "Your Majesty."

The king shook his head. "Of course not, do not get me wrong. I respect anyone who wants to work an honest job, especially for the right reasons. And I know you are trying to prove your capabilities. I assure you, we will give you a fair chance in the coming months."

Those words should have been reassuring, but the meaning behind the reminder of the probationary period rang clear: that if she blew this, then that was it for her. "Thank you, Your Majesty."

"Let's head back then, shall we? Alric will be hungry soon."

They walked back towards the palace, with Poppy keeping her eyes on the path ahead. Once in a while, she would steal a glance at the king. She couldn't help the pang of envy at how King Aleksei obviously adored his son. Not every father did.

Deep in her heart, she knew that Robbie loved Wesley. When he was born, no one had been prouder than Robbie. It was just over the years, he'd focused more on his career and spent less time at home. When he *was* around, all he wanted to do was get Wesley out on the pitch and start playing. Then it had become obvious that their son had no interest in sports whatsoever, and Robbie drifted further away.

It wasn't Wesley's fault.

"Thank you, Poppy."

She'd been so lost in the past that she didn't realize they had arrived in the main palace courtyard. Parking the pram, she turned to him. "You're very welcome, Your Majesty."

The king lifted Alric up and tossed him high in the air, then caught him. The young prince squealed in delight. "I shall see you tonight, my little dragon." He kissed the boy's cheek and handed him to Poppy. "Have a good day, Poppy."

"Thank you, Your Majesty." She took Alric from him, lifting his little hand to wave goodbye as his father strode off into the palace. Turning the prince around, she smiled at her charge. "Ready for some lunch, Your Highness?"

Alric answered with a delighted gurgle.

"Such a happy baby." She placed him back in the pram and maneuvered it inside. As she made her way toward the residential wing, her thoughts turned back to the captain of the guard. *Oh no you don't*, she told her brain—and other parts of her body. She had to remind herself of who she was, where she was, and what she was doing here. Her performance in the next three months would determine the rest of Wesley's life. He needed—no, he deserved the best—best education and the best chance of achieving his dreams. And this job was key to that.

Lusting after some handsome beefcake wasn't going to do her any favors. Besides, it would be unprofessional to even think that way. She had to focus on her work and not be distracted. For her future, and for Wesley.

"Do you have everything?" Queen Sybil asked as she placed Prince Alric in his pram.

Poppy slung the heavy diaper bag over her shoulder. "Yes, Your Majesty."

The queen looked out the window. "Oh dear, looks like it's starting to snow." White flurries fluttered down from the sky. "Are you all bundled up, Poppy?"

"Yes, I'm ready." She pulled on the collar of her wool coat. "I also packed an extra jumper for Prince Alric, just in case." The queen had told her that while the prince had developed one or two of his shifter abilities, until he fully transformed into his dragon, they should treat him like any human child.

"Thank you. All right, let's head out then. We don't want to keep the children waiting."

"Of course, Your Majesty."

Poppy followed the queen as she strode out of the nursery, pushing the pram along. Queen Sybil had explained that every first Saturday of the month she went to visit the Children's Foundation, the local orphanage. However, this was the first time she was bringing Alric with her.

"So," the queen began as they strode down the long hallway that led out of the residential wing. "I just realized this will be your first time outside the palace grounds. I hope we aren't working you too hard, Poppy. At least you'll have your day off tomorrow."

"It's nothing I can't handle, Your Majesty."

In the previous days, Poppy had quickly adjusted to her new job and routine. She began her duties at eight o'clock in the morning when Queen Sybil left for the day. Usually, the prince would be already fed, so Poppy would amuse him by reading him books, playing music, or running around with him in the playroom.

The queen or king would usually come by to visit in between meetings or whatever it was royalty did with their time. Another frequent visitor was Prince Harald, King Aleksei's father. Poppy rather liked the kind older man, who obviously adored his grandson. She was confused, initially, as she knew most kings ascended the throne when the previous king passed away. One of the staffers explained that he'd abdicated and King Aleksei took over, though did not offer an explanation why. In any case, it was none of her business.

In the afternoons, she usually took the prince out for walks outside, though they never strayed too far from the palace. Prince Alric loved the outdoors and often ran away from her the moment she put his feet down in the grass. He really was easy to care for, and as long as he was doing something, generally didn't fuss too much.

Still, running after a toddler was exhausting, and by the time she arrived at her private apartments, she was usually dead on her feet. Wesley, bless him, not only took care of himself for the time being until he started school on Monday, but also had a sandwich and tea ready for her by the time she got home. They'd sit together on the sofa and chat about their day. She told him about what funny things the prince did or what she saw on her outdoor walks. Wesley, on the other hand, usually showed her the books he borrowed from the palace library. Recently, he'd begun talking about his new friend, Gideon, who apparently spent as much time at the library as he did. She didn't question who this Gideon was or who his parents were, but she was happy that Wesley was making friends at last. Overall, she was glad for the distraction, as at least she didn't have time to think of a certain captain of the Dragon Guard.

Well, that's what she told herself, anyway. Sure, when she was busy with Prince Alric or when she fell asleep after a long day, she didn't have the bandwidth to think of anything else. But any other time ... it was like she couldn't stop him from invading her thoughts, despite the fact that she hadn't seen him since that day he'd walked away.

For some reason, the scene played in her mind over and over again. Now, after she'd had time to think about it, she realized she had sounded unreasonably hostile when all he wanted to do was help. It wasn't his fault she couldn't keep her damn hormones in check around him. Maybe she'd apologize to him. If she ever saw him again.

But perhaps she should have been careful of what she wished for because when she walked up from behind the queen, she saw that standing next to the waiting black limousine in the garage was none other than the captain himself. He stood by the open door, back rigid and gaze forward, unflinching even as flakes of white snow settled on him. *At least he wore a top today*, she thought, noticing the all-black wool outfit. It looked like he had trimmed his beard and managed to tame his unruly hair, which only made her want to reach over and muss it all up.

Queen Sybil cleared her throat, making Poppy start. She stopped just in time, a few inches before she hit the queen with the pram. Heat bloomed in her cheeks, and though she tried to open her mouth to apologize, nothing came out.

The queen's lips quirked as her silvery eyes twinkled. "The Dragon Guard clean up well, don't you think?"

"Uh, yes, Your Majesty."

"Even Stein," she said, lowering her voice. "I'm sure he has a soft, mushy inside somewhere that I'm still waiting to discover."

With her attention solely on the captain, Poppy hadn't noticed the other man standing guard by the limo. Though he wasn't as tall as Captain Rorik, he was much bulkier, his shoulders and chest seemingly straining under the black wool coat. With his midnight black hair shaved on the sides and a long, braided ponytail down his back, he looked even fiercer. Poppy couldn't imagine a man like that having any soft mushy parts anywhere.

"Anyway, let's get going, shall we?"

"Yes, Your Majesty." Unbuckling Prince Alric from the pram, she carried him in her arms then waited for the queen to get settled inside the limo before handing him over. She was about to return for the pram when, to her surprise, Captain Rorik already had it folded and carried it with one hand, then placed it in the trunk, all the while never looking at her or meeting her gaze.

"Poppy?" the queen called from inside. "Everything okay?"

"Y-yes, Your Majesty." She climbed in and settled next to the prince's car seat. When the vehicle began to move, she glanced outside, wondering where the two guards were.

"We only have the Dragon Guard with us when we're

outside the palace," the queen began. "They'll be following behind us in their own vehicle."

"Are there many of them? The guards, I mean?"

"There are supposed to be five of them." Her mouth tightened into a line. "But right now, there are four active members. The former captain, Thoralf, is currently away."

The queen didn't offer any further explanation, and Poppy didn't think it was her place to ask any questions, so she busied herself with checking on the prince as they continued on their ride. Soon, the limo slowed and then stopped.

"We're here," the queen declared, and the door opened.

As she stepped out, Poppy noticed the pram was already unfolded and ready. Captain Rorik walked ahead of them, toward the large, white building with columns along the front, while Stein stood by, waiting for them. She took the prince from the queen and strapped him in.

"Welcome, Your Majesty!"

Looking up, Poppy spied someone who was perhaps one of the prettiest women she'd ever seen. Petite and graceful, her stylish heels clicked on the pavement as she walked toward them. Dark chestnut hair fell in waves down her shoulders, framing a delicately beautiful face with high cheekbones, stained pink from the cool air. Her violet eyes sparkled as her gaze landed on the prince.

Brushing away the flakes of snow that gathered on her purple wool coat, she bent down toward the pram. "Oh, there you are, my sweet prince. My, how you've grown," she cooed, then turned to Poppy. "Oh, hello there. I don't think I've had the pleasure."

"Lady Vera, this is Ms. Poppy Baxter, Alric's new nanny.

Poppy, this is Lady Vera Solveigson," the queen introduced. "She's the Children's Foundation's biggest donor, supporter, and champion."

"You flatter me, Your Majesty." Lady Vera offered her hand. "Lovely to meet you, Ms. Baxter."

"Likewise, Lady Vera," she said, taking it.

Lady Vera turned to the queen. "Everything's waiting in the gallery, Your Majesty. The children are so excited to meet the prince. They've been working hard on their presentations."

"That's wonderful! Let's head inside then. I can't wait for the children to meet Alric."

Lady Vera led them into the building, where members of the staff were already lined up and waiting for them, curtseying as they welcomed the queen. They were ushered into a large, airy room where about two dozen children of varying ages sat at tables. When they spied the queen, an excited buzz filled the room, though they all remained in their seats. Queen Sybil waved at them as they walked to the table in front, and once she settled down, one of the staff members came to the stage to begin the program.

Poppy sat next to the queen, with Alric on her lap, watching the various presentations, happily clapping and bouncing the prince along with the songs. Though he probably didn't know what was going on, he nonetheless giggled and cheered and clapped. Once in a while, Poppy couldn't help but feel like she was being watched, especially as she felt a prickle on the back of her neck, though she couldn't figure out who could be watching her.

"Excuse me, Your Majesty," she whispered to the queen as the current presenter—a young man of fifteen who played the violin exquisitely—took his bow. "The prince needs a diaper change."

"Oh." Queen Sybil looked around. "The bathrooms should be down the hallway on the left."

"I'll accompany them, Your Majesty," Lady Vera, who was sitting on the queen's other side, offered. "The program is nearly done, and they'll be setting up for tea anyway."

"Thank you, that would be great."

Poppy got up, picked up the diaper bag, perched Prince Alric on her hip, and silently made her way down the aisle toward the exit.

"It's this way," Lady Vera said, leading her down the long, deserted hallway.

As soon as they entered the ladies' room, Poppy made a beeline for the changing table, pulled it down, and secured her charge. "You don't have to stay, Lady Vera," she said as she unfastened the diaper.

"I don't mind." The young woman's gaze went to the prince, and a wistful smile bloomed on her face. "He's so precious."

She grabbed some wipes from the bag. "Do you have children?"

"No, I'm afraid I don't. I'm not even married," she replied. "And you? Do you have children?"

"Just one. A son, Wesley. He came here with me."

"Oh, how lovely. How old is he?"

"Nine." After she cleaned up the prince, she placed a new diaper under him.

"Nine?" Her mouth formed into a perfect O. "But you're so young. Surely you're not even thirty."

"Twenty-nine. I had him when I was twenty. Way too

young, though, I'm afraid," she said, feeling the corner of her lips tug up. Still, she wouldn't give Wesley back for anything in the world.

When she finished changing Prince Alric, she picked him up and gave him a raspberry on the cheek, making him giggle. "You were such a good boy, Your Highness." Turning to Lady Vera, she asked, "Would you like to have children some day?"

"Yes, I'd love to have children." The smile on her face grew brighter, making her look even more lovely. "Ms. Baxter—"

"Poppy, please."

She nodded. "Poppy, do you think I could ... hold him? Just for a bit."

Lady Vera and the queen seemed to be friends, so she didn't see anything wrong with that. "Of course, my lady." She handed Alric to her. "Let me clean up and then we can head back." As Lady Vera babbled to the prince, Poppy tossed the dirty diaper and wipes into the garbage, then sanitized the changing table before folding it back up.

Prince Alric squealed and wiggled in Lady Vera's arms. "He wants to walk," Poppy explained.

"Ah, right," she said, setting him down. "It's been months since I've seen him, I forget he took his first steps a while back."

"You should hold on to him," she instructed. "Or he'll run away. He's pretty fast, even without his shifter speed. I get winded chasing after him, and my son's a cheetah."

She laughed. "I'll keep that in mind."

They headed out of the ladies' room, Prince Alric in tow. However, when they exited, the hallway wasn't empty as it was when they first came. Right outside the door was Stein, eyes flinty as he stared down at them and his body as still as a rock with his arms crossed over his chest.

Lady Vera huffed. "Oh. It's *you*." Her acerbic greeting didn't faze him, as his menacing expression remained unchanged. "Are you following us?"

"It is my duty to watch over the royal family," he replied, his voice rough and gravelly.

The way they scowled at each other alarmed Poppy, like they were ready to tear each other's throats, so she decided to break the ice. "We were just changing the prince's diaper, Mr. Stein. There was no need to have gone all this way."

"The prince does not leave my sight." His silvery eyes didn't betray any emotion. "And it's just Stein. Not Mr. Stein."

"I—all right. Stein." Clearing her throat, she turned to Lady Vera. "Shall we head back then and take our tea?"

"Yes, let's go." With one last scornful look at Stein, she led Prince Alric away.

Poppy watched as Stein's gaze followed them. *Hmmm.* If she didn't know any better, it wasn't just the prince who didn't leave the severe Dragon Guard's sight. Did she misread their mutual loathing? *Well, it's not my place*, she reminded herself, then followed Lady Vera.

When they entered the gallery, tea had not yet been served, so the children were playing and running around. A small blonde girl with pigtails, probably no more than six or seven, dashed toward Lady Vera, squealing and then wrapping her small arms around the lady's legs.

"*Hei*, Lisbet," she greeted, then bent down to her level. She spoke a few words of Nordgensprak to the girl before switching to English. "Have you been practicing your English?"

"*Ja*—I mean, yes, my lady." Her eyes darted toward Prince Alric. "Is that ..."

"Yes, this is your prince. Can you greet him the way we practiced it last week?"

Her pigtails bounced as she nodded. "It is an honor to meet you, Your Highness," she said before executing an adorable curtsey.

Prince Alric smiled, reached out, and tugged at the colorful straps of her dress.

"I think he likes you," Lady Vera said with a chuckle. "I—oh!"

It seemed they caught the rest of the children's attention, and now, about a half dozen of them crowded around Lady Vera, all wanting to get closer to the prince.

"Cease!" came a loud growl from behind.

Poppy's head whipped back and she saw Stein rushing forward, seemingly intent on getting to Prince Alric. Without a second thought, she put herself in his path. "What the bloody hell do you think you're doing?"

Stein's jaw hardened. "I must protect the prince."

"Protect him? From what? Those adorable orphans?" *Was this man insane?*

"What's going on here?"

Her skin went all tingly at the sound of the familiar voice. *Oh, for God's sake.* Him. She spun around, arms stiff at her sides as she curled her hands into fists. But she must have miscalculated how close he was because his solid body collided with hers, sending her backward. She braced herself for the fall, but a pair of strong hands gripped her arms, pulling her back onto her feet. "I—" *Oh dear.* She shouldn't have looked up. Those eyes. They stared down at her, boring into her very being, making her feel like there was no else in the room. No, scratch that. No one else on earth. He was so close that—

"*Ahem.*"

The captain released her at the sound of Stein clearing his throat. He blinked and then looked at the other Dragon Guard. "What's happening?"

"I was about to evacuate the prince when Ms. Baxter stopped me," he groused.

It was as if a cold bucket of water had been poured over her head. "Evacuate ... are you crazy?" She disentangled herself from the captain's arms.

"Calm down, Ms. Baxter," Captain Rorik said. "He's just doing his job."

Calm down? The condescension in his tone only rankled her. "Doing his job? They're just *children*! They aren't going to harm the prince. Do you know nothing about kids?"

"What's going on here?" Queen Sybil's hushed tone was neutral, though her lips pursed together tightly. She raised a brow at them, but didn't say a word. Captain Rorik looked at Stein, then back at the queen.

Poppy frowned as the silence stretched out. *Am I missing something?*

Finally, after Rorik nodded, Stein let out a breath. "As you wish, Your Majesty." He bowed, then turned on his heel and marched out of the gallery.

What in God's name was going on?

"Please see to Prince Alric, Poppy," the queen ordered. "Lady Vera looks overwhelmed."

Glancing over at Lady Vera, she saw that the young woman did look frazzled as more children swarmed her and the prince. "Yes, Your Majesty. And m-my apologies." Oh God, this was her first public outing with the prince, and she'd screwed it up. *I shouldn't have let Lady Vera just take him.* She couldn't help it; Lady Vera had looked so happy holding him earlier.

She glanced back as Queen Sybil and Captain Rorik continued ... whatever it was they were doing, staring at each other. *Eyes straight ahead,* she told herself. Hopefully this little mistake wouldn't be a permanent mark on her record. Oh God, surely the king would hear about this incident. What would he think?

A knot grew in her belly. Now, more than ever, she had to concentrate on her work. She couldn't afford any more missteps. And she definitely could not afford any kind of distraction, no matter how good-looking or tempting.

CHAPTER 4

The great blue water dragon rose out of the water, its horned head breaking past the frothy waves as it soared up. Rorik steered his dragon toward the shore, hoping the time they spent in frigid waters of the Norwegian Sea had been enough to cool the creature's temper.

In the past two weeks, its mood swung between melancholic and displeasure. Since the incident at the Children's Foundation, Rorik had kept away from Poppy, especially after the queen's chastisement.

Queen Sybil had not been pleased with any of them for nearly causing a scene. As captain, Rorik had to walk a fine line between serving his queen and letting his men know that he would always have their backs. *Stein saw the prince being swarmed and Lady Vera being besieged,* he had reasoned with Queen Sybil. *He was only performing his duties.*

While she did not defend Poppy for leaving the prince with Lady Vera, she did not spare Stein either. *You have to remember where we are,* she had told him through their mental link. *I appreciate you taking your duties so seriously, but there was no need to shout at the children. If you cannot act reasonably around them, then perhaps another member of the guard should accompany me on my visits here.*

Of course, he didn't tell the queen that Stein would never allow that. Ever since her monthly visits to the orphanage had been placed on the official schedule, Stein had made sure he would be the only one taking that particular job. Rorik didn't care as long as the assignment was covered, and with them being short-handed anyway, it worked out better. He usually didn't accompany Stein and the queen, though that day, he told himself his presence was necessary because the prince would be there as well.

His dragon snorted.

Oh, quiet down.

He'd always lived in harmony with his dragon. Indeed, it was one of the lessons his father had imparted on him. That relationship with his animal had helped him become a great warrior and Dragon Guard. But now, his mate's presence had caused turmoil between them. It could not understand why they just couldn't claim their mate now. But how could he, when with each passing interaction, Poppy only seemed to detest him more.

The dragon hung its head limply.

He landed on two human feet right by where he left his clothes by an outcropping of rocks. As a fabled shifter, his clothes shifted with him, and he didn't need to take them off, however, he preferred to jump into the surf in human form first so he could feel the prickly cold salty water on his skin before he eventually shifted into his dragon. Besides, his clothing more often than not ended up sandy and wet after a swim anyway, so it was easier to just take them off.

After he dressed, he fished his phone out of his pocket. An unread message blinked on the screen from Gideon. *Huh.* It was seven o'clock in the evening, so he should have been off duty by now.

Please come to the library as soon as possible. I need to speak with you about that research on Zaratena I'm doing. I'll be here until eight.

Zaratena. *Right.*

A few weeks ago, the royal family had gone back to Blackstone, Colorado, to visit the queen's hometown. A Christmas ball had been held in their honor, and the king's great-aunt from the human side of his family, Princess Natalia of Zaratena, had been in attendance. Somehow, the princess had convinced the king to help her find a long-lost member of the family, and then assigned the task to Rorik. Having not the faintest idea where to begin, he decided he would have to learn more about Zaratena so he could work on his next steps.

While Rorik welcomed any task given to him by his king, it was one more thing the Dragon Guard had to add to their list of duties, not to mention, it seemed they were no closer to finding the cure for the wand than they had been when Thoralf went off on his quest. He wanted Thoralf to succeed so his friend could restore the king's dragon and his own honor, but he did secretly want the former captain to come back and take up the mantle of leadership again.

With a deep sigh, Rorik placed the phone back in his pocket and made his way back to the palace. At least Gideon was on task. But then again, he enjoyed research and the pursuit of knowledge anyway.

Rorik entered the library, making his way past the rows and rows of leather-bound books and headed to the large wooden table in the middle of the cavernous room. A figure sat, head down, engrossed in some weathered tome.

"Gideon?"

The scholarly dragon looked up, amber eyes focusing. "Rorik. Glad you got my message." He nodded to the chair in front of him. "I finally found the time to compile my research. And seeing as you're busy with your duties, I thought I'd just give you the summary, but I'll send the report to your desk in the morning as well."

He plopped down on the wooden chair. "Thank Odin." Gideon's considerate and sensitive nature made him a good addition to the Dragon Guard, and they often relied on his knowledge and computer skills. In fact, part of his training had been on cybersecurity, and the previous king had even given him permission to leave the Northern Isles to complete a computer science degree at CalTech. "So, what can you tell me?"

"Zaratena," Gideon began, turning the book he was reading to face Rorik, "was a country in the Baltic region, approximately here, somewhere between Latvia and Belarus." His finger landed on a map on the yellowed pages. "They were quite prosperous for hundreds of years and ruled by the Royal House of Tsarevich, but six decades ago, they were overthrown by revolutionary forces. They installed a parliament, but without any clear direction and much infighting among the leaders, the country collapsed less than twenty years later and the land was absorbed by neighboring countries."

"And the royal family? What happened to them?"

"The king and queen, unfortunately, perished in the revolution, leaving behind three children. As you know, their middle son, Prince Maxim, had been living here in the Northern Isles trying to establish diplomatic relations when the revolution broke out. When the news came out about the collapse of the monarchy, King Hagar, grandfather to our current king, granted him refuge. He married one of our local nobles, and their daughter married the then-Crown Prince Harald and became mother to our King Aleksei. Meanwhile, the only daughter, Princess Natalia, escaped to Russia and married Igor Dashokov."

"And the heir to the throne?"

"According to all witnesses, reports, and Princess Natalia herself, Crown Prince Ivan died along with his parents. The princess, along with Ivan's wife and child, the Grand Duke Aleksandr, were supposed to escape together to Russia but became separated in the chaos. So, all this time, he'd been presumed dead."

"They had a member of the Dragon Guard with them, correct?" Rorik asked. "He was assigned to the Royal House of Tsarevich." It must have been a great honor for the king of Zaratena to have a dragon to guard him and his family. "Who is he? From what house was he from."

Gideon's golden brows knitted together. "That's why I asked you to come right away. You see, I don't know."

"What do you mean, you don't know?"

"I mean, there doesn't seem to be—"

"Gideon!" came a call from behind. "Gideon, where are you?"

Rorik swung his head around at the sound of the unknown voice. To his surprise, a small figure zoomed toward them, before stopping short a few feet away. He immediately recognized the young boy whose dark eyes widened as they landed on him. Excitement turned into anxious energy as he took a step back.

"Wesley," Gideon greeted. "It's rather late for you to be coming here. How are you enjoying school?"

The boy didn't say anything, though he swallowed loudly. A wave of nervousness emanated from him.

"Wes? Where are you?"

Now *that* voice, Rorik knew. His dragon, too, recognized it and immediately lifted its head.

Poppy rounded the corner and walked toward them, wrapping her cardigan tightly around herself. "Wesley, did you—" She stopped, too, as they locked gazes. "What are you doing here?"

He should be asking that of her but held his tongue.

Gideon pushed up from his seat. "Wesley, have you met Rorik? He's the captain of the Dragon Guard. I guess you can say that makes him my boss," he joked.

The boy shrank further, backing up into his mother. Poppy placed a protective arm around him. "Wesley, I thought you said you wanted to introduce me to your friend, Gideon. Where is he?"

Gideon chuckled. "Hello, you must be Wesley's mum. I'm Gideon."

As the other man approached Poppy and Wesley, Rorik's dragon immediately went on alert. It did not approve of another unmated dragon near her.

Her brows knitted. "You're—oh, I didn't realize ... when Wesley said he made a new friend, I thought he was another kid." A rich laugh escaped her lips, and she smiled up at him.

Two deep dimples appeared on her cheeks, making her look even more youthful and lovely.

A deep stab of jealousy hit Rorik straight in the chest because he realized that this was the first time he'd seen her smile, yet it was not for him.

His dragon let out a roar so loud, Gideon stiffened and turned to him, eyebrow raised. *Everything all right, Rorik?*

I—I'm fine.

Shrugging, he turned back to Poppy. "I hope you're not disappointed."

"N-no, not at all. I'm Poppy, by the way." She offered her hand, and he shook it. "Nice to finally meet you, Gideon. You're all Wesley talks about."

"Gideon's the coolest, Mum," Wesley began. "He says he's read every book in this library."

"Nearly," Gideon corrected.

"I want to read every book here too," Wesley continued. "And Gideon says he's going to lend me his personal copies of the *Adventures of Halfdan the Mighty* once I can read in Nordgensprak."

"It was written by one of our most prolific and beloved authors, Erik Forberg," Gideon said. "I've read all thirty-three of his books numerous times. Unfortunately, he died a few years ago, but his was one of the first books we had translated into English. So far, the National Library has only released the first three volumes."

"I've already finished the first one, but I'm devoting an extra hour of study every day to learning Nordgensprak," Wesley said proudly. "So that I can read them all in the original language."

Poppy laughed again, a sound that should have brought

Rorik joy, yet the jealousy only deepened. "That's very kind of you, Gideon. And if those copies are your childhood treasures, I can assure you Wesley will take very good care of them. He became terribly cross with me when I broke the spine of his copy of *The Hobbit*."

"Ah, Tolkien." Gideon's expression turned wistful. "One of my favorites."

"Mine too," Wesley beamed.

This was all too much, and Rorik wanted—no, needed—to get out of here. "If you'll excuse me, I should get going."

Gideon frowned. "But I'm not done with telling you about my research. The Dragon Guard—"

"It can wait," he bit out. "Good night." Turning on his heel, he marched toward the exit. His dragon seethed, unable to bear the sight of Poppy and Wesley with Gideon. Had he forgotten about her son?

Do you know nothing about kids?

Her words still stung every time he replayed them in his head. Poppy being a single mother was not an issue for him or his dragon. He would care for Wesley as he would for her and be whatever she needed him to be to her son. Wesley was important to her and he respected that.

Yet, twice now, he'd shown his incompetence around younglings, first, by scaring her son and then, defending Stein. It seemed in her eyes, he could do nothing right, and that was perhaps what wounded him the most.

Rorik, came Gideon's voice in his head. "Rorik!"

Halting, he spun around and saw the other man jogging up to him. His dragon roared at the sight of the rival male, remembering the look of adoration on Wesley's and Poppy's faces when he spoke of his beloved books.

"What is it?" Rorik spat. "If this is about the Dragon Guard in Zaratena, I told you it can wait." When he turned his back and attempted to walk away, Gideon merely used his shifter speed to get in front of him.

Amber eyes regarded him. "It's not about Zaratena."

His patience was running thin. "Then what is this about?"

Gideon folded his arms. "I don't know. You tell me, Rorik. Why is your dragon ready to tear my head off?"

"It is not," he said through gritted teeth.

"Is that so?" He snorted. "You know, Wesley tells me his mother and father have been divorced for five years now and that Poppy's never had a boyfriend since then. Bet she's all ripe and ready for the picking for the first man who—"

Fury rose in him. "Scoundrel! You will cease such talk or I will rip your tongue out!" Grabbing Gideon by the neck, Rorik slammed him against the wall. His dragon was ready to burst out of his skin and shred Gideon to pieces for even speaking that way about their mate.

Mine, it roared. It was so loud he couldn't stop it from broadcasting through the mental link.

Gideon let out a choke, but managed a smile. "I ... thought ... so."

The red cloud of rage ebbed away, and he released Gideon. "Oh, Yggdrasil ... Gideon ... my friend ... I am sorry." Shock sent a chill through him.

"It's ... all right." Gideon cleared his throat as he rubbed at the bruise on his skin. "Tell me ... Poppy ... is—"

"She's mine," he whispered hoarsely. "My mate."

"And you've known this—"

"Over a week now, since she arrived."

"What?" he exclaimed. "Does she know? Why haven't you done anything?"

"I tried, but there hasn't been any chance for me to do so." He recounted to Gideon everything that occurred since Poppy and Wesley arrived. "She does not care for me, and I can understand why."

"Rorik, that's not true."

"And you know her? Know what's in her heart?" Ugly jealousy reared its head again.

"What I mean is, if she's your mate, then she must feel something for you. Attraction or a pull of some sort." Gideon paused. "Maybe you should ask the king—"

"No!"

"No? But he is the only one among us that is mated and therefore can tell you what to do. Or you can ask the queen—"

"Absolutely not."

"But why not? I mean, all right, I understand it's a private matter, but then, what steps are you taking to win her over?"

He rubbed the bridge of his nose. "I'm not sure ... I don't know if I should even do it."

"I beg your pardon?" Gideon asked incredulously. "You're not going to claim her?"

"Shhh!" He glanced behind Gideon. What if Poppy heard them?

"Don't worry, they both came to look for books and are very much occupied." Gideon placed a hand on his shoulder. "Rorik, finding your mate is a special thing. Not all of us get such a chance. How could you even think of not claiming her?"

"She does not want me." His dragon cried out in protest. *It's true. She despises us.*

"She does not *know* you," he retorted. Slipping a hand around his shoulder, he gently led Rorik back toward the library.

"What are you doing?"

"Since you are too stubborn to go after her, then I shall give you a push in the right direction." Steering him inside, he dragged him to the end of the library. "She should be down there." He gestured to the row nearest the end. "She's looking for books about the history of the Northern Isles. I shall keep the boy occupied in the fiction section, so *go to her*." To emphasize, he gave Rorik a push.

"I—alright." His throat suddenly felt dry as a desert, but he managed to take a step forward. That's it, he told himself. Just one step forward. It was like when he was learning to shift into his dragon or fighting with a new weapon. He just needed to take the first step.

Slowly, he made his way to the history section. As he turned the corner, he slowed, then stopped. Just as Gideon had said, there she was, scanning the titles on the shelf. An ache built in his chest at the sight of her. Even dressed simply in leggings and a green cardigan, she was the most elegant and beautiful woman he'd ever seen. A dark green bandana held her curly hair away from her face, and the overhead lighting played on the planes of her profile and bathed her face in a glow, making her skin look like burnished copper.

Engrossed in her search, she didn't notice his presence. Lifting her head, she scanned the shelf, then reached for something on the top one. She had to tiptoe to reach it, but even then, her fingers only skimmed the spine.

Clearing his throat, he caught her attention.

A soft gasp left her lips, and she took a step back. "You ..."

"May I be of assistance, Ms. Baxter?" With careful steps, he approached her. Though her eyes widened, he didn't sense any fear or apprehension. "Or I could ask Gideon to bring you the ladder? I'm sure there must be one here somewhere."

She hesitated for a moment, then gestured to the shelf. "If you wouldn't mind."

His dragon bobbed its head up and down, seemingly claiming victory. *Calm down*, he said. *We are only retrieving a book for her.*

"It's, uh, the one at the end there. *The Concise History of the Northern Isles.*"

He saw the book and deftly took it out. "Here you go," he said, handing it to her.

She accepted it and hugged it to her chest. "Th-thank you, Captain Rorik."

"You're very welcome. And please, it's just Rorik. No one calls me captain."

"Oh." Her brows drew together. "I'm sorry. Was that a mistake? The queen called you the captain of the Dragon Guard."

"Yes, that's my designation, but it's not really a formal rank. But you committed no error, so there is no need to apologize."

"I see ... thank you, Rorik."

His heart wanted to burst out of his chest at the sound of his name on her lips. "You're very welcome."

"Well, thanks again." She sidestepped him. "I guess I'll—"

"Ms. Baxter, one moment. If you please."

She froze in place, her shoulders tensing. However, she did turn her head toward him. "Yes?"

"If I may ... I would like to apologize for my conduct during the visit to the orphanage."

"Oh." Her lips parted. "There's no need—"

"Yes, there is. And for Stein as well."

Her lips pursed. "He's his own man."

"Yes, but as his captain, he's my responsibility when he's on duty. Stein is ... he's not used to being around children or know how to act around them." And with his childhood, he couldn't blame Stein. But that was his story to tell. "And frankly, neither do I."

"You don't have ... children of your own? Or a wife?"

"No."

"Siblings?"

"I grew up an only child."

"Oh." Her arms lowered, and she tucked the book to her side. "Me too."

"Yet you are good with children. The prince especially. It's probably because you're a good mother."

"Oh, well ..." Her lashes lowered. "I was a primary school teacher and Wesley, well, I'm learning everything about being a mum from him, though it's probably cheating because he's such an easy kid."

"He does seem to be bright and intelligent." Though a tad timid.

"I ... I'm sorry as well if I haven't been nicer or friendlier, and I overreacted to Stein doing his job. I just don't know what it's like around here, how to act, how things work, and what's proper." She took a deep breath. "This job ... I really need it. For me and for Wesley."

"And I embarrassed you in front of the queen last Saturday, putting your prospects in danger." She didn't answer, but he knew that was it. He kicked himself mentally, as did his dragon. "So, I do owe you an apology."

"No, I—"

"Please. I'll accept your apology if you do mine."

She lifted her head to meet his gaze, a smile slowly spreading across her face. "All right. Apology accepted."

"Same." His lungs squeezed, making it difficult to say anything else. She grew even lovelier as her dimples deepened. It was such a simple gesture, and not the first one he'd witnessed, but there was something different about this particular smile.

She gave him a nod. "Perhaps we could start again. Not as friends or anything—"

"Yes, friends," came the immediate answer from his lips. *An excellent idea.* That was how they could get to know each other, as friends first.

"Oh." She shifted in her stance. "I mean, we don't have to ... but if we could just be ... er ..."

"I mean ... if you are unsure of what to do or how things work around here, you may call upon me. Anytime. That's what friends do, right?"

"Er, yeah."

"Then I would be happy to assist you and guide you, Ms. Baxter."

"I guess that would be nice. And please, call me Poppy."

"All right ... Poppy."

They stood there for a few seconds, though before the

awkward silence settled in, she said, "Well, I should really get going. Wesley probably has homework ... or something."

"Of course." He stepped aside. "Have a good evening, Poppy."

"You too, Rorik."

He watched her retreating back, and once she disappeared from view, he leaned back on the shelf and let out a breath. That knot in his chest all but disappeared, and a warmth replaced it. Oh, Freya, what he wouldn't give to be close to her again, to breathe the same air she did, or even get a whiff of her scent. And that smile ... he knew now why it was so different. Sure, it was shy and tentative, but this time, it was all for him.

His dragon, too, felt aglow from their mate's attention, though it kicked its tail in impatience.

Calm down, he said. *At least she doesn't despise us any longer. Things will be better from now on.*

It huffed at him, in an approximation of what Rorik translated as *I hope so.*

CHAPTER 5

"Is that all better, Your Highness?" Poppy fed Alric the last spoonful of mashed peas, which he happily gobbled up. "You were just hungry, weren't you? You're a growing boy, I should tell your mum that you need to eat more for breakfast."

This morning when Queen Sybil had handed him off to Poppy, Prince Alric had been more fussy than usual and eventually threw a full-on tantrum before the queen could even leave. While Queen Sybil had been distraught, Poppy told her that she would take care of the prince. After about an hour of playing, she realized what was wrong—Alric had just simply been hungry.

"Hello, knock, knock."

Poppy turned her head and saw Prince Harald standing in the doorway. "Good morning, Your Highness." She curtseyed. "I'll have him ready for you in one second. He just needs a quick cleanup." She wiped down Alric's chubby cheeks and hands, then unstrapped him from the chair.

"There you go," she cooed, handing him over to Prince Harald. "You be good for your grandpa now."

The older prince's face lit up as Alric reached for his beard and tugged. "My, my, you're growing so strong every day, my boy."

"Thank you for offering to watch over him while I go to my meeting," Poppy said. "I appreciate it."

His gaze did not leave his grandson, who was now tapping him on the chest with his little hands. "Not at all, Poppy. I love spending time with Alric. Now, go or you'll be late."

"Thank you." With another curtsey, she headed out the door. Now, where was she supposed to go again? *Ah, right. The queen's office, west wing, ground floor.*

Before she left this morning, Queen Sybil had given her some news: The royal family would be embarking on a European tour in a few weeks. There would be a planning meeting this morning, and the queen wanted her to be there since she would be traveling with them.

Poppy was apprehensive at the thought of traveling so soon after she had just arrived, but it wasn't like she could say no. Hopefully she could find someone who could look after Wesley while she was gone.

Of course, that wasn't the only thing on her mind this morning. Running into Rorik yesterday had unnerved her. After about a week of not seeing him, she thought she was fine and had gotten over her attraction to him. But it seemed it only hit her with a harder force this time.

Oh Lord. He'd looked so yummy, and they'd been standing so close together alone in that library. Plus, he'd apologized for his behavior. She even couldn't remember the last time Robbie had said sorry for anything.

Not that she was comparing, because after all, Rorik said he just wanted to be friends.

Ouch.

"Well, I did suggest it first," she said aloud to no one in particular.

But he didn't have to agree so fast.

True. And she did tell herself that this was for the best. No way was she going to act on her impulses around the captain of the Dragon Guard. Really, he wasn't even *that* attractive.

Liar, liar, pants on fire.

Poppy slapped herself on the forehead. *I need to stop having conversations with myself.*

As she arrived at the queen's offices, she pushed all thoughts of Rorik and her impulses away. The young woman waiting at the reception desk outside directed her to the conference room to the side and Poppy entered. "Your Majesty, I'm—oh." *Oh, dear.*

Sitting to the queen's right at the conference table was the object of said impulses. Rorik looked up at her, then flashed her a bright smile. "Good morning, Poppy."

Her temperature spiked a few degrees as his low baritone caressed her skin like a lover's touch. "Uh, hello, Rorik. Er, and, Your Majesty."

"Poppy, come in." Queen Sybil gestured to the chair beside Rorik. "Thanks for being early. We're just waiting for everyone else so we can begin."

She did as she was told and sat down. Rorik glanced at her

and smiled again before turning back to the queen. Wiping her hands down her trousers, she glanced at him. He was wearing his all-black coat again this morning with his hair slicked back neatly. Yesterday, he'd been more casually dressed in the loose linen shirt she'd seen him in that first time, though it had been damp, and she remembered he smelled of seawater and sweat. God, the way it clung to his shoulders—

Damn impulses.

Sitting up straight, she took a deep breath. Silence stretched on with just the three of them, and though only seconds ticked by, it seemed an eternity.

"Oh, dear," Queen Sybil exclaimed. "I'm sorry, Poppy."

"Pardon me? For what, Your Majesty?"

"We've been excluding you from our conversation."

"Huh?" She glanced around. Had she been so consumed by her wanton thoughts that she didn't realize they were speaking?

Ooh, you deserve time in horny jail for that one.

Oh, shut up.

"We have been using our mental link to communicate through our thoughts," Rorik explained.

"Mental link? Like telepathy?"

Queen Sybil nodded. "Yes. Dragons of the same species can use telepathy over short distances, though as Aleksei's bonded mate, I too can use it to communicate with him and the Dragon Guard."

"I didn't know shifters could do that." Would Wesley be able to do that? Did he already do it?

"Not all shifters," Rorik began. "Just fabled shifters."

"Shifters who turn into mythical creatures, not real ones," Queen Sybil interjected. "I didn't know there was a difference until I met Aleksei either. It's a long story, I'll tell you about it some time."

So that's what was happening the other week at the orphanage. "So, you can have whole conversations without speaking aloud?"

"We shouldn't do it in front of other people," the queen said. "It's rude. At first, when I was learning to do it, I practiced all the time, and now it's a force of habit."

"How interesting." Poppy had never heard that there were different classes of shifters before, much less that they had different powers.

The queen glanced toward the door as people began to file in. "Ah, looks like they're here."

As soon as everyone gave the queen a proper greeting and settled themselves, Melina went to the opposite end of the table, across from the queen.

"Good morning, Your Majesty, everyone, and thank you for coming here," she began. "We're here today to give a preliminary overview of the upcoming royal European tour. I know some of you were surprised to hear that we have moved up the dates, but due to scheduling conflicts, we won't be able to start in the late summer as planned." The lights dimmed, and then a projector flashed a map behind her. "So, to begin. ..."

Melina talked for about an hour before she answered some questions. When she finished and no one else spoke, she clapped her hands together. "All right, seeing there are only a few weeks left to plan, we must make haste and get to work. Your Majesty, is there anything you'd like to add?"

"You've done a wonderful job, Melina, thank you," the queen began. "And to all of you, thank you for coming today and I know we can all work to make this tour a success. This is going to be a challenge, having to organize everything on such short notice, but I have every faith in all of you." She nodded at the door. "You're all dismissed."

Everyone stood up, but the queen caught her eye. "A moment, Poppy?"

"Of course, Your Majesty." She sat back down. Rorik glanced at her and hesitated for a moment, then left the room along with everyone else.

When they were finally alone, Queen Sybil spoke first. "First of all, you're not in trouble or anything."

She let out the breath she'd been holding. "Oh, good. What can I do for you, Your Majesty?"

"I wanted to speak to you about the schedule. That you'd be all right with it."

"M-me? I mean, it's my job, Your Majesty. I go where the prince goes, and I assume I'm here now because you'll want me along."

"Yes, of course, but I was thinking of Wesley. You know, the first week of the tour coincides with the school's half term break, so I made sure to have Melina start in London so you can bring him along. Then if you want, he can do remote learning for the week, or he can come back with some of the staff and stay in the dorms with the other students who board."

"Oh, that's very generous of you, Your Majesty." Her parents would be thrilled at seeing Wesley again, plus he'd probably want to go to all his favorite places. "Thank you."

"No problem. Perhaps Wesley's father could spend time with him. He must miss Wesley a lot."

Oh, right. *Robbie.* "Er, yes." As if Robbie would give a

damn. "I'll have to let him know." *Yay.* She was so looking forward to contacting her ex. *Not.* Still, part of their custody agreement was that she had to let him know whenever they were coming to London so he could see Wes.

"And finally, there is something else I must tell you. Something that will perhaps affect your job as well." The queen chewed at her lip. "The real reason we're pushing up the date of the tour isn't due to scheduling conflict. I mean, it *is* because of a scheduling matter ... you see, I, uh, just found out that I'm pregnant again."

Poppy gasped. "Truly, Your Majesty? Why, that's wonderful!"

"Thank you." Queen Sybil placed a hand on her belly. "Aleksei and I are thrilled. But, aside from our families and the Dragon Guard, only you know. We're trying to keep it a secret until after the tour, but you can see why we can't do it in the summer. I'll be due around end of July."

"Of course. Congratulations, Your Majesty." Oh, a baby! How exciting. It had been a long time since she'd held an infant, and it was only at this moment she realized how much she missed it.

"Two babies ... I don't know how I'll manage. I was thinking it was too soon, but, well, it just happened." A wrinkled appeared between her brow. "By the way, how is Alric? Did he stop crying after I left? Was he sick?"

"Oh yes, he's fine." She clapped her hands together. "It was nothing, Your Majesty. The prince was merely hungry."

"Hungry? But I fed him as soon as we got up."

She tapped her chin. "Hmmm, if I recall, Wesley started eating more right around that age as well. His body is preparing for his first shift and needs more calories."

"Really? Oh, thank God, I thought I did something wrong. Thank you, Poppy." Queen Sybil massaged her temple with her thumb and forefinger. "I don't know how you do it."

"Do what, Your Majesty?"

"This ... the parenting thing." She slumped back in her chair. "I don't know if I'm doing things right, and I'm so afraid of making a mistake. What if I do something wrong and I ruin him? There's so much pressure on me and raising my son right because someday he's going to be the king."

Poppy's heart went out to the young woman. Right now, Queen Sybil looked vulnerable and lost, a feeling that she, and perhaps millions of mums everywhere, could relate to. "Your Majesty," she began. "I hope I don't overstep my bounds here, but if I may speak candidly ... I may not have the same responsibilities as you, but as a mother, I do know how you feel. I've felt that pressure, just as you have, like everyone is watching every move you make and waiting for you to make a mistake."

"Y-you have? But you're so good at it. And Wesley's such a wonderful boy."

Poppy couldn't help the chuckle that escaped her mouth. "I truly lucked out with him. But, the thing with raising children is, you can wish and beg and plead and do everything in your power to make them to turn out the way you want, but no matter what, in the end, they can only be themselves." There was that pang in her heart again, the same one she felt when she thought of Wesley and his relationship with his father. Robbie did everything he could to mold their son into his image, but still, Wesley could only be who he was.

"What do we do? Why even bother parenting then?"

"That's the question, isn't it?" She sighed. "I ... I think we just need to do our best and love them for who they are." Her throat burned, and she wished she could give Wesley a hug right this moment. "It's all worth it, though."

The queen sat up straight and took a deep breath. "You're right. You're so wise, and I'm very lucky to have you, Poppy."

"Thank you, Your Majesty."

"And if things go well, I hope you'll consider staying on with us for a long time. Assuming the king agrees, of course."

Excitement fluttered in her chest at the thought of what that meant. Years of job security and school fees for Wesley. Maybe he could even go to Harvard like her father did. But that would all hinge on her performance in the next couple of weeks. "If I were to be lucky enough, I'll gladly stay."

"I'm sure you'll do great."

"Thank you. If that is all, Your Majesty, I should go back and see to His Highness. I don't want to impose on Prince Harald any longer."

"Don't worry, I'm sure Pappa and Alric are having a grand time right now. But yes, thank you. You may go."

Getting up, she curtseyed to the queen and made her way out. To her surprise, waiting outside the door was Rorik.

"Poppy," he greeted with a wave of his hand.

Oh God, her hormones went into overdrive again. *Bloody hell.* And she'd done so well during the meeting, ignoring his presence as he sat beside her. "Er, Rorik. You're still here."

"Yes, uh." He rubbed the back of his neck with his palm. "I was waiting for you."

"Waiting for ... me? Why?"

"So I could speak with you."

"Speak with me?" *Oh God, I sound like an idiot.* "What about?"

"I was wondering if we could ... if I could see you later tonight, after you are done with your duties?"

Giddiness surged inside her. "Yes," she blurted out. *Oh, yes.* "I mean, that would be fine."

"As colleagues, of course," he added. "I would like to ask for your assistance on the matter of the tour."

His words quashed the giddiness. What did she think he was doing anyway, asking her out on a date? "Of course. But, er, what can I help you with?"

"This is first tour the royal family has done in ... well, ever, as far as I can recall." He scratched at his chin. "There will be many protocols that must be created and rules to enforce. You are from London, correct?"

"Yes, though I've mostly lived in the northern part."

"Perhaps you can tell me more about the city and give me the lay of the land. I'm sure I could find the information in guide books or online, but as a native Londoner, you might be able to impart some key information I won't find elsewhere."

"I suppose I could try, but I'm no expert."

"You know more than me," he pointed out. "And, well, it would really help me out. My job as captain of the Dragon Guard is quite demanding, and I don't have much time to sift through maps and guidebooks. If you could give me an overview, that would at least give me a good place to start."

"I see." She supposed that made sense. "Of course I'll do it. Happy to."

"Excellent. How about we meet at the library tonight? What time is good for you?"

"Six thirty?"

"Thank you, Poppy, you're a good colleague and a good friend."

"No problem at all," she said through a tight smile, despite the fact that the word *friend* sent a bruising blow to her ego. "I should get back to the prince ..."

"Of course." He nodded at her, then turned on his heel and walked away.

Poppy watched him go, feeling relief when he disappeared out the door. Yet, she couldn't help the excitement bubbling up in her. *Get a grip.* This was a work meeting, nothing more. And she was here to do a job, not hook up with one way too hot and way too out of her league dragon shifter.

Despite reminding herself that she had to stay cool and be professional, Poppy couldn't help the anticipation building inside her as she not-so-very patiently waited for six thirty to arrive. She kept glancing at her watch every five minutes, willing the hours to go by faster, and by the time the queen arrived to dismiss her, she practically flew out the door.

After a quick dinner, she and Wesley were now on their way to the library. She had told him she needed to do some work as well and that he could tag along. It was a work meeting, after all, and definitely *not* a date. Unsurprisingly, he did not object and seemed as eager as she was. That is, until he saw Rorik standing by the door.

"Poppy, Wesley," he greeted, his mouth widening into a smile. "Good evening."

"Good evening, Rorik." Her pulse thrummed in her veins. Wesley, however, shrank back and held onto her hand, then pressed himself against her side. "Wes," she warned gently. "Rorik just said good evening to you."

He murmured something that sounded like hello, but then shrugged and glanced away. "Can we go in now? I want to see Gideon."

The heat of embarrassment crept up her neck, and she gave an apologetic glance to Rorik. "Er, shall we head in?"

"Of course." He gestured for them to walk inside first.

"Wait, he's coming too?" Wes frowned up at her. "Why?"

"I told you, I have some work to do."

"With *him*?"

"Yes," she said, exasperated. What was going on with Wes?

Thankfully, Gideon approached them, and Wesley released her hand and flew toward him. "Gideon! I've finished the second—" He skidded to a halt and glanced behind the dragon shifter. "Whoa!"

A second man stepped up from behind Gideon. A … second Gideon?

"Hey, you must be Wes," Gideon Two said, bending down to Wesley's level. "I'm Niklas, Gideon's brother."

Wes's jaw dropped. "Uh, hi," he said shyly.

Standing up to full height, he turned his attention to Poppy. "And you are?" His dark amber eyes twinkled, and she saw something in them that she never saw in Gideon's —interest.

"I'm Poppy, Wes's mum."

"Hmmm … you don't look like any mother I know. Ow!" He glared at Gideon, who had kicked him in the shin. A few seconds passed, and Poppy guessed they were probably doing that mental link thing. "Er, I mean, nice to meet you, Poppy," he mumbled.

"What are you doing here, Niklas?" Rorik asked. "The library is that last place I'd expect to find you. Don't you have places to be? Perhaps one of those bars or clubs in town to trawl?"

"Ouch, Rorik, you wound me!" He put a heart over his hand. "I asked Gideon to go hang out with me, but he said he was busy. When he told me he was here because you asked him to help—Yeow!" That earned him another kick in the shin, and this time, a freezing stare from Gideon and Rorik.

"Rorik, I've placed those maps and books about London for you in the reading room," Gideon motioned toward the rear of the library.

"Ah, yes, we should get started. I would not want to keep you too late, Poppy, especially as this is your leisure time."

"Yeah, sure. Let's go then." Wesley's hand, however, tightened around hers. "Is there something you need, Wes?"

"I—" His nostrils flared. "Nothing."

"All right then, have fun with Gideon and Niklas."

As Rorik led her away from the trio, Poppy couldn't help but think about Wes's strange behavior. He was borderline rude to Rorik, and if he kept this up, she may have to have a talk with him about his attitude. While her son was mature for his age, it was way too early to be starting those rebellious teen years.

"Is everything all right?" Rorik asked as they walked down a row of shelves.

"Yeah ... I'm sorry about Wes. I mean, he's not usually so rude. Shy, yes, but never rude."

"Ah." He seemed to ponder on her words. "I can sense his cub's anxiety each time we meet. His cheetah, I mean."

"Really? Like what do you mean by sense?"

"It's difficult to explain, but when shifters are in the same room, even those who are of different types, their animals give off an energy. Creatures in the wild do this as well. If he's not been raised around others of his kind, then his cheetah might feel anxious around shifters, especially those who are bigger and more dominant."

"That makes sense." She chewed at her lip. "When I found out Wes was a shifter, I did all the research I could. There wasn't much information available online, though I did exchange emails with another human mum who married into a pack of wolves in Venezuela. I received a lot of help from her, though she did warn me wolf cubs are different from cheetah cubs."

"I know you have done your best."

"You do?"

"Yes, of course, you said—I mean ... I'm sure you have. Anyway, shall we?" He gestured farther down to the door at the end.

"Right."

She followed him inside the reading room where a table was piled high with books and maps. They sat down, and she pulled out one of the large guidebooks. "Okay, let's begin...."

The minutes went by as she gave Rorik an overview of the London Metro Area, highlighting important places that the king and queen might visit or would want to request to see.

"So, Piccadilly Circus isn't a real circus?" Rorik asked.

She thought he looked adorable with that confused look

on his face. "No, it's a busy crossroads with lots of interesting architecture and billboards and tourists. Have you never been out of the country?"

He shook his head. "I'm afraid not."

"Oh, are you not allowed to leave?"

"It's not that," he said. "Some may think us isolationists, but we are a self-sufficient country and have everything we need here. And, yes, maybe partly it is for our protection. Dragon shifters, in general, prefer to keep to ourselves and stay out of the limelight."

"I did notice that I couldn't find a lot of information about the Northern Isles and dragons in general."

"Yes, that's mostly because the Dragon Council—that's the alliance of all the dragon clans in the world—has many rules about what can and cannot be publicized about us. We are already few and far between."

"Why is that?"

"Because we've been hunted down." His jaw hardened. "Humans and other kinds of shifters have killed many of our kind due to their prejudices, fear, or they think our bodies have special magical powers. In the Middle Ages, for example, ground up dragon shifter bone was thought to cure the Black Death. So, our numbers have dwindled over the last few centuries, plus dragons don't produce a lot of offspring, and we can only have dragonlings with another dragon or human partners."

"Oh, I'm so sorry. People can be so terrible." And she knew firsthand how cruel they could be to those different from them, but she never thought anyone would do real harm to Wesley. "If you don't mind my asking …why can't dragons produce a lot of offspring?"

"I am not sure. Perhaps it is nature's way of preserving balance. Here in the Northern Isles, for example, we have ten dragon families and only about fifty dragons in total."

"Only fifty?" She thought the place would be teeming with dragons and that every other person on the street would be a dragon. "I thought there would be more of you. Who else lives here then?"

"Our population is mostly humans and a few other types of shifters. And also, we have not seen a female dragon in over a century."

"Really? There aren't any female dragons here except for the queen?"

He paused, like he was going to say something, but changed his mind. "There are no female water dragons currently living in the Northern Isles."

"Wow. Fifty male dragons." An absurd idea came to mind as she thought of those dating shows that were so popular a while back. "Maybe you should open up your borders and start some kind of dating tourism scheme. I'm sure they'll be swarming this place when they find out there are fifty hot male dragon shifters." She gasped and covered her mouth. *Oh, holy Christ!*

Rorik didn't seem to have noticed the meaning behind her words or her embarrassment. "Well, truthfully, I would say only half of those are eligible bachelors. Most are already mated to human or shifter women, and that count includes the young dragonlings like Prince Alric. And those who you would consider 'eligible' serve in the Dragon Navy or Dragon Guard."

"Like you?" *Oh fuck.* She slapped herself mentally.

When would this word vomit stop? "And, uh, Gideon and Niklas. And Stein," she managed to add.

"Yes," he said. "We aren't forbidden to find ma—wives. But serving our king keeps us busy."

"I'm sure you'll find someone who would understand the demands of your duties." *Someone young and pretty, and could give him a dragon baby*, she added glumly.

"Well, uh ..."

"Wait, do you have someone? Someone in mind at least?"

"I, uh ..." His entire face turned red. "Not ... quite."

Her heart plummeted. *Yes, there was.* She could see it in his face. It reminded her of when Wesley was younger, and he tried to hide something naughty he'd done.

"I mean, if there is ... it's not a big deal. I mean, it's great!" Her voice squeaked unnaturally. "You should, go after her and stuff."

She was about to wish for the floor to open and swallow her up when Wesley's face popped in through the doorway. "Mum?" His gaze darted to Rorik briefly before settling back on her. "Can we go now? I have homework I need to finish."

"Yes!" She shot up, and the chair's legs made a screeching sound as it scraped across the tile floor. "I'm, uh, sure you've got a good overview of the city now, Rorik. I marked the books where there might be some important information you'd like to do further reading on."

"I shall come back and look through the pages you marked. Goodnight, and thank you, Poppy."

"Sure. Anytime." As casually as she could manage, she waved to him but didn't meet his gaze, though she could still feel his eyes on her as she and Wesley walked off.

"What did he want?" Wesley asked.

"He just needed some help, that's all."

"With what?"

Oh dear, she'd forgotten to tell Wesley about the tour and the trip to London. How would he react? "Well, um, why don't we head home and I can tell you more?" A pit grew in her stomach. Wesley was just settling into school and now she was going to take him out again, not to mention, go and meet with Robbie. But this was her job, and she couldn't leave him alone during his half term break.

"All right." Before they left the library, he waved to the twins, who were standing by one of the shelves. "Bye Niklas! Bye Gideon! See you tomorrow."

"Tomorrow?" she asked as they walked out. "Are you coming back here tomorrow?"

"Gideon said he'd be doing some extra research this week, so I asked if I could come after school and do my homework here."

"Oh."

"Is that okay? I promise I'll get everything done and be back at the flat before you arrive."

She ruffled his hair. "Of course, Wes, and I know you will. But, uh, don't you maybe want to spend time with other kids at school? Have you made any friends there?"

"Gideon is my friend," he said defensively.

"I know but ..."

"Is Rorik *your* friend?"

She halted and placed her hands on her hips. "And what is that supposed to mean, young man?"

"I dunno," he shrugged. "I'm just asking."

She worried at her lip. "I *am* glad you have a friend, Wes."

"Gideon is cool," he said with a sniff. "You should hang out with us. Maybe we can all get dinner or something."

She looked at him suspiciously, then decided to use the two words parents used when they didn't want to make promises they couldn't follow through on. "We'll see."

CHAPTER 6

Rorik was rather proud of how the evening turned out. Spending time alone with Poppy had been exhilarating, to say the least. To have her so close by pleased his dragon, too. This was an excellent first step in winning her over.

Sure, he had not been 100 percent truthful; though her information was helpful, he didn't truly need it as the tour's planning committee would take care of the details. But he remembered something his father said when he trained Rorik in combat: If an opportunity should open up to gain an advantage, one should seize it.

Perhaps this wasn't what Neils had in mind with the lesson, but nonetheless, he saw an opportunity and grabbed it with both hands.

After stacking the books neatly, he picked them up and went back out to the main library hall. "Gideon?" he called. "Where should I return these books?"

"Well, well, now," Niklas began as he narrowed his gaze

at Rorik. "That was interesting. What were you two doing back there all alone?"

His dragon roared in his ears loudly, snapping its jaws at Niklas. "We were working."

"Working, huh? Did you get some tutoring with the hot new nanny?"

Rorik was about to drop the books and lunge at Niklas, but noticed the corners of his mouth tug up. Gideon, meanwhile, suddenly found the wainscoting interesting as he avoided Rorik's gaze. "He knows?"

Gideon looked up at him guiltily. "Er, sorry, Rorik. But you know how he is."

He rubbed the bridge of his nose. Unfortunately, he did know what Niklas was like when it came to ferreting out information. *Like a dog with a bone.*

"And you didn't tell the rest of us that you found your mate?" Niklas said in a mock hurt tone. "I thought we were brothers in arms!"

"It is a private matter," he stated.

"Tsk, tsk, Rorik." Niklas strode over to him and patted him on the shoulder. "You should have come to me first. I could have given you some pointers on how to woo a woman."

"Somehow I doubt we have the same definition of 'wooing' a woman," he said wryly. "And she's not just any woman. She is my mate."

"*Pffft.*" Niklas crossed his arms over his chest. "She's still female, right? And if she is your mate, why are you wasting time playing footsie with her in the library?"

"I am not wasting time." His dragon, however, didn't

agree and shook its horned head. "I am merely getting to know her first. We agreed to be friends."

"*What?*" Niklas exclaimed, raising his palms in the air. "Friends? Are you kidding me?"

"No. And why would I? Should mates not be friends as well? The king often mentions how Queen Sybil is his best friend."

"Yes, but he's not stuck in the friend zone."

"The what?" Rorik asked. "What is a friend zone?"

"Oh, pipe down, Niklas, there's no such thing as a friend zone," Gideon interjected. "Women are complex beings who don't just place men in certain categories."

"Right, and tell me again when your last relationship was? Have you even talked to a woman recently?" When Gideon remained silent, Niklas snorted. "Yeah, I thought so. Rorik," he continued. "Once a woman gets to know you 'as a friend,' you'll likely end up in the friend zone. That means she sees you *only* as a friend and she won't want to have sex, er, have a romantic relationship with you for fear of ruining your friendship."

"What ... is that truly possible?" He didn't think that when Poppy offered her friendship, that he was going into the 'friend zone' forever.

"Yep," Niklas confirmed. "Trust me. I know."

Rorik scrubbed a hand down his face. "Odin's beard, what have I done?" If only he had more experience with romantic relationships. Or *any* experience, for that matter. Most of his life had been devoted to his training, then his duty as a Dragon Guard. He thought that eventually, he would find a wife and sire an heir for their house, but that was far into the future. For now, there was no time for forming attachments, not when his king depended on him. "Is it too late?" His dragon did not like this situation one bit. It clawed at him, urging him to do whatever it took to claim their mate.

Niklas cocked his head to the side. "Hmm, hopefully not."

"I don't see why we can't ask King Aleksei for help," Gideon said. "That seems to be the most logical way to go about this. He's the most experienced out of all of us."

"The king has enough on his plate." The Dragon Guard weren't just King Aleksei's most loyal protectors, but his closest friends as well. Last night, the king had gathered them together and made the announcement that the queen was expecting again. They had drinks and raised their glasses to him, the queen, and the new baby. Rorik had never seen King Aleksei so happy, except maybe the last time he announced Prince Alric's impending arrival. This time, though, there was a pang of envy in Rorik's chest, as he, too, wished for what the king had. A family of his own.

"Every woman is different," Niklas began. "What worked for him might not work for you. You need to get her alone, away from work, and just romance her."

"Romance her?" He frowned. "How am I ever to do that?"

"You just need the right atmosphere, where she's relaxed and she can get to know you in a more casual setting. Ah-ha!" He snapped his fingers. "I have an idea."

"You do? What?"

"It's our birthday this weekend," Niklas said. "Gideon and I will throw ourselves a party at Aumont Park. We'll invite everyone, including Poppy."

"We will?" Gideon asked, perplexed.

"Yes, it's a great plan, don't you see? We'll have music, dancing, drinks. Poppy can bring her son along, and we'll distract, er, babysit him while you go and romance her."

It sounded like a good plan and he could see the merit in it. Within the palace walls, they were employees of the king and queen, bound by their duty to serve. But perhaps if they could spend time outside where they were just themselves, she could see him in a new light—and take him out of the friend zone. "Let's do it then." His dragon roared in approval.

"Great! I'll take care of everything." Niklas gave him an encouraging squeeze on the shoulder. "Just you wait. Maybe by this time next week, you'll be bonded and mated too. Now, I gotta go get planning. See you guys later."

As he watched Niklas walk off, Rorik shook his head. "That was unexpected. I didn't realize your brother was a romantic."

The corner of Gideon's mouth twisted upwards. "Let me tell you a secret. Most people think Niklas is this playboy heartbreaker because he's got a new woman on his arm every couple of months. But the truth is, he's always the one getting his heart broken." He shook his head. "He falls in love way too easily and ends up hurt in the end. And while you think he'd learned his lesson, each time he just picks himself up and gets right back at it."

Huh. Niklas always projected himself to be a fun-loving, devil-may-care lothario. Rorik never knew he was a sensitive romantic at heart. Indeed, he expected that from the more introverted Gideon.

"Anyway, if you don't want to go through with this hare-brained plan, then we don't have to have a party," Gideon said. "If you want to do things your way, I'll help you out. You can keep meeting with her here, if you like."

"No, that won't do. I could keep asking for her advice, but eventually, I'll run out of excuses. Niklas's plan is worth a try to perhaps get me out of the friend zone." For now, he would avoid Poppy, just in case. He didn't want her to further think he only wanted friendship from her. Somehow, he would have to prove himself a worthy male, and if Niklas was right, he'd win her over, and they could finally be bonded mates.

CHAPTER 7

"Hey, guys! Nice to see you both. Glad you could make it!" Niklas greeted as Poppy and Wesley walked in through the doorway. "Welcome to Aumont Park."

"Thanks for inviting us." She couldn't help herself as she glanced around the huge, richly decorated foyer. "And for sending the car to bring us here. Happy birthday!" She handed him the brightly wrapped package in her arms.

"Of course! And aww, thanks, you didn't have to." He took the gift from her. "Hey, Wes, how's it going? Is that for Gideon?" He nodded at the similar-looking package in the boy's hands.

Wes's mouth was hanging open as he looked around the room. "Are you guys rich or something?"

"Wes!" But she couldn't blame him. When the sleek black car that had picked them up from the palace turned the corner and began to drive towards the sprawling French-style stone mansion, she had been stunned herself. And it was even more magnificent on the inside.

Niklas laughed. "It's all right. House of Aumont is one of the more prosperous dragon families in the Northern Isles, thanks to my ancestors. They had a rare talent, you might say." There was a twinkle in his eye, but he didn't elaborate further. "Anyway, c'mon, the party's started, and we have lots of food and drinks. Gideon's been waiting to show you our library, Wes."

"Wicked!"

"Your house is amazing," Poppy said as they walked through the high-ceilinged halls filled with art on the walls. "I didn't realize you lived so far away from the palace though."

"This is our family's ancestral seat and where Gideon and I were raised," he explained. "But as members of the Dragon Guard, we live full time on the palace grounds. Our housing isn't as swanky as this, but it's nice too."

He led them inside, giving them tidbits of information about the house before finally leading them outside to an enormous lawn where a huge white canvas tent had been set up. As they approached the entrance, the two uniformed men standing guard opened the flaps to let them in.

"Oh," she exclaimed. "It's warm in here."

Niklas helped her with her coat, then handed it to the counter just beside the entrance. "Yeah, well, we couldn't have an outdoor party in this weather unless we only wanted shifters to come. But this heated tent is the next best thing."

"It gorgeous inside too."

Swathes of cloth crisscrossed along the ceiling, while lanterns and fairy lights added a cozy atmosphere to the interior. Tables and chairs were set up, music blared from speakers, the dance floor filled with people, and buffet tables heaved with food.

"Poppy! Wesley, glad you could make it!" Gideon waved as he came up to them.

"Happy birthday," Poppy greeted.

"I got this for you." Wes held the gift up to him. "Well, Mum paid, but I picked it out."

"Thank you both," he replied, taking the gift. "Come on, you must be hungry. Let's get some food and sit down."

Gideon ushered them to the buffet table and helped them pile their plates with food, then sat them at one of the empty tables as Niklas came with glasses of wine for the adults and lingonberry juice for Wesley.

"You have so many friends," Poppy remarked, glancing around them.

Gideon smirked. "Niklas has many friends."

"Aww c'mon, bro. It's your birthday too, you know. Everyone's here for the both of us."

Everyone except Rorik, Poppy thought. But she wasn't surprised the captain of the Dragon Guard wasn't here because he'd been missing the entire week.

Not that she was looking for him.

She thought that maybe he needed more help with planning for the tour, so she went to the library the day after their first meeting. Disappointment had filled her when he didn't show up. But she told herself that perhaps he was busy with other things. But when she went again the next day and the day after that, there was no sign of Rorik.

She sighed inwardly. *We're just work friends.* Colleagues at this point, really. Did she ask too many personal questions? *I must have made him uncomfortable.* Yes, that was it. Or he'd taken her advice and gone after that girl he was obviously in love with.

Her stomach tied up in knots thinking of him with another woman. But it wasn't like she had any claim on him.

"I wonder where Rorik is?" Niklas said aloud.

She started at the sound of his name, but caught herself and took a sip of her wine.

"Gideon, may I see your library after I'm done eating?" Wes asked.

"Of course—"

"I said," Niklas sent a meaningful look at Gideon. "I wonder where Rorik is."

"I—oh right." Gideon scratched at his chin. "I think he said he was going to be late. Had some last-minute preps to take care of. I'm sure he'll be here soon."

Poppy downed her wine with one gulp. "I think I'll go get another drink."

"Here, let me," Niklas said, signaling one of the waitstaff.

"No, no." She waved him away and got up. "I need something stronger." Though her party girl days were behind her, she did once in a while indulge in a stiff drink or two. Besides, it had been a long time since she'd gone to a party that didn't involve overly sweet cake and clowns. Striding over to the open bar, she caught the bartender's eye. "Vodka martini, please."

The man leaning against the bar beside her turned around. "Hello there." His tall, lean frame towered over her, and his blond hair glinted under the glow of the party lights overhead.

"Um, hello."

Startling blue eyes assessed her. "I don't believe I've seen you before ... your accent ... are you English? New to the Northern Isles?"

"Yes, I am. And I moved here a few weeks ago. How did you guess?"

A smile formed on his handsome face. "The Northern Isles is a very small place, and I know almost everyone who's anyone here."

"Well, I'm not anyone," she said, then nodded gratefully at the bartender who slid her drink forward. She took a sip and closed her eyes as the alcohol slid smoothly down her throat and warmed her belly.

"A woman as beautiful as you? I doubt that."

The warmth crept up to her cheeks. Oh, this guy was definitely flirting with her.

"Where are my manners?" He tsked. "I'm Lars of House Aumont."

"Poppy Baxter." She held out a hand. "I, uh, work with Gideon and Niklas. And how do you know them?"

He took her hand, his palm warm and grip firm. "Gideon and Niklas are my cousins."

"Oh." She should have seen the resemblance. They had the same hair and fine features, though the eyes were different, and he looked at least a decade older than the twins. That meant he was probably a dragon too. "Nice to meet you, Lars."

"So, Poppy, you work at the palace."

"Yes." She took a sip of her drink to avoid having to explain. It's not that she was ashamed of her position, but she did sign a bunch of NDAs before flying over here, so she actually couldn't just tell anyone what she did and who she worked for. "And you? Are you part of the Dragon Navy?" She recalled Rorik telling her that most of the able-bodied dragons were part of the Northern Isle's naval force.

"I was, but now I'm only in the reserves, called upon in case I am needed. I leave the heroics to my twin cousins. I'm afraid I only look after the family interests."

From his very expensive suit and watch, Poppy could guess they were very big interests.

"Cheers." He lifted his drink. "To new friends."

She grimaced at the word. *Friends.* Another friend was the last thing she needed. However, as she clinked her drink to his and watched him over the rim of her glass, a thought popped into her head. Lars didn't work for the royal family, therefore, she could flirt with him and there wouldn't be any conflict of interest or interference in her duties. Besides, she'd clocked out hours ago and miles away from Helgeskar Palace. She was on her personal time, and she could do whatever she wanted.

Needing more courage, she gulped down the rest of her drink before placing it back down on the bar. "Do you dance?"

"I beg your pardon?"

"I asked if you danced." She cocked her head toward the dance floor. The music had changed to one of a slower tempo. "Well, would you like to dance?" Whoa, that vodka martini gave her more than a little courage.

He held out his arm. "Shall we?"

Hooking her arm into his, she allowed him to lead her out to the dance floor. His hand settled on her waist as she slid her palm up to his shoulder and linked their other hands together.

"I should thank my cousins for inviting you here. I can't remember ever being asked to dance."

She chuckled. "Seriously? Is the Northern Isles stuck in

the past? It's the twenty-first century. Women should be allowed to ask men to dance."

"I fully agree, but then again I'm biased because I have the most beautiful woman in my arms."

"Flatterer."

"Only if it's not true."

He spun her and the combination of the motion and alcohol made her dizzy. His arms wound around her to steady her. "Oh my ..."

"Perhaps we should sit down?"

"No," she purred. "I want to finish the dance."

And so, they continued dancing with Lars holding her close, chatting about nothing in particular. When the music wound down, they slowed to a stop. "How about we get another drink and maybe find somewhere more ... private? I grew up here at Aumont Park and know all its secrets."

"I—"

"Poppy."

The low baritone made her spine stiffen. Slowly, she turned her head "R-Rorik?"

He stood—no, loomed over them, arms at his sides. Poppy's stomach did a flip at how handsome he looked in a casual gray suit jacket and trousers, his dark shirt open at the collar to show off his tanned throat. His face, however, turned down into a scowl as a menacing aura surrounded him.

"If it isn't the captain of the Dragon Guard," Lars said. "Nice to see you, Rorik."

"Lars." Rorik's tone was tight. "I'm sorry I'm late," he said to Poppy. "I had to make sure the palace was secure in my absence."

She shrugged. "You should apologize to Gideon and Niklas, not me. Shall we head out, Lars?"

"Where are you going?" Rorik growled.

Lars's gaze moved from Poppy to Rorik, then back again. "Why don't I go ahead and give the bartender our drink orders? Just meet me there when you're ready to go."

Poppy gawked at Lars as he scampered away. If she didn't know any better, she would have guessed that he had been scared off. But what could have—*oh*. Whirling around, she faced Rorik.

"Ready to go?" he echoed. "Are you leaving with him?"

"Did you say something to him? With that telepathy of yours or something?"

"What? No," he denied.

"Then why did he run off like a scared rabbit?"

Rorik's brows drew together. "How should I know? What were you doing with him, anyway?"

"What was I doing?" She blew out a breath. "We were just dancing, that's all."

"And then what? Were you going to sneak off somewhere for a private dalliance," he sneered.

She gasped. "I beg your pardon? Who the hell do you think you are? How dare you judge me for what I do on my personal time, especially after you've avoided me for these last few days."

"Avoided you?"

"Yes! I went to the library every night, hoping you'd be there and—" *Uh-oh.* She clapped both hands over her mouth. Damn vodka! He stared down at her, eyes wide, but said nothing.

Embarrassed, she did the only thing she could think of—

run away. She ignored the stares of the people around her as she darted toward the exit. Unsure where to go, she turned right, rounding the humongous tent and making her way across the lawn. Her thin dress and tights barely protected her from the biting cold, but she didn't care.

When her lungs burned and her legs couldn't carry her further, she stopped, bending over and heaving as she attempted to inhale as much oxygen as she could.

Oh God, how was she ever going to face him? Admitting to him that she's been waiting for him was bad enough, but running away made it worse. Why did she say those things? His snub this last week just felt so deliberate, and it had hurt. *I shouldn't have expected more. I shouldn't have—*

"Poppy."

A large shadow hung over her, but she didn't have to guess who it was. Slowly, she lifted her head.

"Poppy," he repeated, taking a step toward her. "I'm sorry. For ignoring you."

"No, it's fine." Standing up straight, she tugged at the hem of her dress to straighten it. "You don't have to apologize."

"I should. I see that now." His hand raked through his hair, mussing it up. "I just ... I was trying to ... I did not want to be your friend. That's why I stayed away."

Her stomach dropped. "Oh. Right. I understand, totally. We don't have to be friends."

"No!" He muttered something unintelligible under his breath. "That is not what I meant."

"Then what did you mean?"

"I ... I do not want to be in your friend zone!" he blurted out.

"I beg your pardon?" Did she just hear that right? "Friend zone?"

"Yes. You know, that place where a female deems a male unsuitable as a romantic partner."

The words coming from Rorik's mouth nearly made her giggle. Friend zone? Really? "Wait, do you mean you don't want to be there? In the ... friend zone?" Moisture gathered on her palms.

He took a step forward. "I do not wish to *just* be your friend."

"Oh." She blinked. "*Ohhh.*"

Intense green eyes bore into her, blazing with an emotion that sent her heart pattering like mad. She wasn't sure who made the first move. Did he wrap his arms around her first, or did she throw herself into them? Anyway, that and any other questions didn't matter as their lips melded together in a searing kiss.

The cold dissipated around them and was replaced with a heat that shot straight to her core. His lips devoured hers, his tongue seeking entrance into her mouth. She obliged, opening up to him, their tongues dancing together.

A hand slipped under her dress, and she moaned into his mouth as his warm hand slid up her belly and rib cage to cup her breast, his fingers finding her nipple over the lace of her bra cup and teasing it to hardness. She pushed against him, wanting to feel his body against hers. Her arms wound around his neck to bring him closer. A knee nudged her thighs apart, and he hauled her to him, making her straddle his leg. The friction it caused made her melt against him, her body shuddering as she slid along his body.

It was everything she wanted, everything she could only

dream about, and his mouth and hands told her it was the same for him. Her body tightened, and she wanted more, her peak nearly there—

Oh God! Poppy pulled her mouth away and disentangled herself from him, taking a step back, the heat leaving her body. His eyes still blazed with passion, his chest heaving as he took deep breaths.

"I ... I'm sorry." Realization swept over like a cold wave, sobering her. She couldn't do this. Ever since she met him, this almost seemed inevitable, but her brain kept telling her she had to resist.

"Sorry?"

"I just ... I can't," she choked out. "We shouldn't have."

"I don't understand." His face was a mask of confusion. "I thought you wanted—"

"I do! I mean ... Rorik, we can't do this. We work together, this is just not professional."

"Professional?"

"Yes. I mean, I need this job." Her voice shook. "I can't risk it. Wesley, he wants to go to this boarding school in England, and this is the only way I can afford it. We were nearly homeless when I lost my job a few months back, and now I have this chance, and if Queen Sybil decides I can stay, I can pay for his school fees until he goes to university."

He remained silent, though his shoulders sank.

"Please, I have to be a good mother to him. I can't be selfish." No matter how much she wanted Rorik, she had to think of Wesley first. "Please say something."

His jaw ticked, but he gave her a short nod. "I ... understand. And I'm sorry. I shall not ... bother you again."

Something draped over her—his jacket. "Rorik?"

"You are shivering." He took a step back, then spun on his heel.

She watched him go, disappearing into the darkness. Closing her eyes, she took a deep breath. His jacket was still warm from his skin, and trace scents still there. Musky and male and all *him*.

A loud flapping startled her, which was then followed by a piercing shriek. The energy crackling in the air told her he'd shifted into his dragon form. Lifting her gaze high, she saw the shadow of something large and winged soar overhead, then fly off.

Oh, Rorik.

She didn't mean for it to go that far. That kiss ... her lips still burned at the memory, her body left wanting at the loss of him. It was the alcohol, she told herself. And it was a good thing she came to her senses before—

She couldn't think of that, of what could have happened. She had to remind herself of why she was here. With Queen Sybil expecting another child, it could mean her job would be secure for another few years. The queen all but told her she wanted her to stay for both children, but that would all hinge on the king's approval. And surely, he wouldn't approve of a nanny who slept with other household staff.

Another shiver went through her, and she snuggled deep into the jacket. *This was for the best.* She made her way back to the tent, hoping no one would notice she'd been gone. It was too warm inside, so she slipped the jacket off. Folding it in her arms, she gave it one last deep sniff before handing it to the coat check counter.

Her eyes scanned the place, then she breathed a sigh of relief when she couldn't find Lars anywhere. *Thank goodness*. It would have been awkward to have to talk to him after what happened. She thought he was attractive, but compared to Rorik he was just so ... lacking. Sleeping with Lars would have been a bigger mistake.

Straightening her shoulders, she headed back to the table where Wesley and Gideon were still sitting together. "Hey, guys," she said, trying to sound casual.

"Poppy." Gideon looked at her strangely. "Is everything all right?"

Did he see her confrontation with Rorik? Probably, based on the way he seemed to search her face. "Yes, everything's fine." She sat down on the empty chair next to Wesley. "Just fine."

CHAPTER 8

The next three weeks passed in a whirlwind of activity, and Poppy was glad for the distraction. Aside from planning for what Alric needed, she also had to prepare for herself and Wesley. He wasn't all that thrilled about leaving school and going back to London to see his father, but at the same time, he didn't want to be without her for such a long time.

So, they compromised and decided he would come along during the break and then go back to the Northern Isles when school re-started. It worked out because he would be accompanied by Gideon, who would be on duty that entire first week before heading home to swap places with Niklas. Wesley would then stay in the dorms with the other kids who boarded for that last week, and Gideon even promised to check in on him every day.

Surprisingly, getting in touch with Robbie and scheduling a visit had been the easiest part of planning the trip. They would only be in London for the first three days, so they agreed to meet on the afternoon of the second day.

There was so much to be done before they left that Poppy felt relief the moment they left the palace for the airstrip. She and Wesley would be traveling with the king, queen, and prince in their private plane. The flight was only three hours long, but the moment they arrived in London, they would pretty much be up and running.

"Are you excited to stay at Buckingham Palace, Wesley?" Queen Sybil asked.

"Yeah, it's cool," he said. "I've been to the outside a couple of times to see the changing of the guard, but never inside."

"We'll be seeing a lot of the inside," Poppy chuckled. Thankfully, King Aleksei and Queen Sybil would be doing most of the heavy lifting throughout the tour, and except for a few key events, she and Prince Alric would mostly be staying indoors.

"I brought a lot of books. I shouldn't run out," he stated.

"Well then—oh." The queen looked up, her face lighting up. "You made it, I thought we were going to have to leave without you."

King Aleksei bent his head as he walked in through the small doorway. "And would you leave me and go off on your own, *lyubimaya moya*?" He grinned. "The Prince of Wales is happily married, but I wouldn't blame him if he left his future queen for you."

Queen Sybil rolled her eyes, but the blush on her face made her seem years younger.

As the king walked toward them, another figure filled the doorway. Poppy wasn't surprised at who it was. She'd prepared for this moment after all. As captain of the guard, Rorik would be with them throughout the tour, and the moment they left the Northern Isles, he would never leave the king and queen's side.

She had thought she was ready to see Rorik again, even practiced the cool, polite expression she would put in place whenever he was around. But her traitorous little heart rattled an uneven rhythm in her chest and her stomach flipped at the sight of him in an expensive-looking dark suit, crisp white shirt, black tie, and aviator sunglasses. Thankfully, he turned to face the front of the plane and settled into the first seat by the door.

She'd never had hot bodyguard fantasies before, but she was pretty sure she was about to start having them now. *Gah.* She gripped the armrests of her chair.

"Mum?" Wesley elbowed her.

"Huh? I mean, yes?"

"You should fasten your seatbelt. I think we're about to take off."

That wasn't the only thing about to take off.

Oh God, that horny voice was back.

"Um, right." She buckled her seatbelt and leaned back. This was going to be the longest two weeks of her life.

Poppy had to admit, being able to stay in the Belgian Suite at Buckingham Palace was a great perk of the job. She also got to meet the queen and the Prince of Wales, albeit briefly when the Northern Isles staff was presented to them when they arrived. It was nerve-racking, as though she'd lived in England most her life, she had never actually seen any member of the royal family in real life. She was glad that that was the only function she would have to attend, at least, until the next destination on the tour.

While the king and queen were out and about, she spent most of the day unpacking Prince Alric's things and settling into the sumptuous suite. When she had a few minutes, she called her mum and stepdad, who were so excited that they would have brunch tomorrow. She also fired off a text to Robbie to confirm their time and meeting place. The only reply she got was a "k."

Still, if he didn't show up, it wouldn't be a loss. She'd already done her share of comforting Wesley when his father "forgot" to pick him up for his visitation days, and after a while, he only shrugged and asked to be taken to the library.

The following day, she got up early, prepared and briefed Ingrid, the reliever nanny, and then woke up Wesley so they could head out.

Brunch with her parents was fun, and she didn't realize how much she had missed them until now. They, too, obviously missed her and Wesley, and they eagerly listened to his stories about the Northern Isles, living in Helgeskar Palace, school, and of course, the library and his friend Gideon. Throughout the morning, though, her stomach tied up in knots, dreading the afternoon with Robbie, but she tried her best not to think about that.

When they finished their meal, they headed to the science museum and spent a few hours there looking at the dinosaur fossils and other exhibits. But by two o'clock, they had to get going.

After saying their goodbyes to her parents and promising to call before they left England, she and Wesley walked up a few blocks to the Primrose Cafe and Tea shop. Much to her surprise, Robbie was already outside. But he wasn't alone. There was a young woman with him—very young, Poppy observed. *Was this girl even out of uni?* She hung on his arm and tossed her long blonde locks as she giggled at something he said.

Poppy cleared her throat to get their attention.

They pulled apart, and Robbie, as usual, had that stupid 'I'm not doing anything wrong' face. "Hey, Pop," he greeted. "Wesley! There's my buddy!" He bounded over to them and ruffled his hair. "How are you? I missed you!"

She stared at him, agog. His buddy? *Missed* him? Did she land on a different planet? A different dimension?

Wesley's mouth pulled back into a thin line. "Who is she? And why is she taking my picture?"

The girl—er, woman, had her phone out and had it pointed at Robbie and Wesley. "Aww, don't you two look adorable? What a sweet reunion."

"Oh, yeah. Come here, babe, let me introduce you." He gestured for her to come over. "Guys, this is Chablis."

Poppy frowned. "Chablis?"

"Yeah, like the wine." Chablis tottered over to them in her sky-high stiletto heels. "Mum and Dad wanted something classy." She held out a hand. "You must be Poppy, nice to meet you. And you"—she bent down, her tiny skirt riding up her thighs—"must be Wesley. How are you, luv? Aren't you glad to be back in England?"

"Right." Wesley's gaze narrowed. "Who are you exactly?"

Poppy nearly choked trying to suppress her snicker. "Um, Wes, that's rude." *Good boy*, she added internally.

"Chablis is, uh, my intern," Robbie said with a nervous laugh. "She's helping me out with a few things."

Intern? *Suuuure.* "How nice." Poppy forced a smile on her face. "So, do you want to head inside?" She cocked her head toward the tea shop.

"Oh, yeah!" Robbie placed an arm around Wesley. "Let's go buddy. Are you hungry? Let's get some cakes and scones."

She let them go inside first, making sure to hang back a bit. This was Robbie's time with Wesley, so she didn't want to interfere too much.

"I'll get us a table." Glancing around, she found an empty table with four chairs. Honestly, she should have left them, but she knew Wesley would likely freak out if she did. Besides, there was nothing in their custody agreement that stated they had to be alone. In his previous visits, Robbie never minded having her hang around as that meant he could cut out early without having to wait for her to come back.

Drumming her fingers on the table, she watched Robbie hover and fuss over Wesley as they looked at the display case and menu. *Huh, maybe Robbie did miss him.* Absence made the heart grow fonder, right?

Of course, she couldn't stop rolling her eyes as Chablis photo-documented every single moment, even taking a few selfies with Robbie and Wesley. *Oh God, she's one of those people.* Poppy had a phone, and she took photos of Wesley and herself, but she didn't need to document every single minute. Maybe Chablis was just excited because she wasn't used to being around children.

Except those her age, that voice inside her said in a snide voice.

She couldn't help the giggle that burst from her mouth.

"Everything all right, Pop?" Robbie asked as they approached with a tray of food and drinks.

She cleared her throat. "Um, yeah."

"I got you your favorite." He handed her a cup of Earl Grey tea. "A touch of milk and sugar."

"Thank you." Robbie could really be sweet and thoughtful when he wanted to be. In fact, he was, all the time in the early days. He never forgot her favorite flowers or her birthday. It was only later that he'd changed. And maybe so did she in some ways.

"So, Poppy," Chablis began as she sipped on her latte. "Robbie tells me you work abroad as a nanny! How exciting."

"Er, yeah. It's boring though. I mostly stay indoors with the baby all day." No one back here knew who she was working for, of course. "So, what do you do, Chablis? Aside from being Robbie's intern?"

"I work at the Crimson Cave—"

"She's a waitress," Robbie added with a nervous laugh. "Now, how about these scones?"

Poppy bit her lip. Oh, she could guess what the Crimson Cave was. And what Chablis did. Not that she judged the other woman for her choice in career; if she wasn't hurting anyone, Poppy didn't care. *But, really, Robbie?* Did he have to bring a stripper to his meeting with his son? She shot her ex a glare, but he didn't seem to notice.

Well, it's his life. And she had no say in it, not anymore. At least he was trying to build his relationship with Wesley, if the way he fussed and catered to their son right now was any indication.

However, history had told her that there was something not quite right here. But what? And perhaps she wasn't the only person feeling that way. Wesley was quiet and withdrawn—more so than usual, and he only spoke in monosyllabic words while avoiding Robbie's gaze. Poppy knew she shouldn't have ignored her gut, and that became more evident as the day wore on and they moved from the cafe to a park nearby.

"Hey, Wes! How about a bit of rugger, eh?" Robbie asked as he took a rugby ball out of his backpack.

Oh God, not this again. "Robbie, no." She looked at Wesley, whose eyes had grown wide at the sight of the ball. "It's okay, Wes, you don't have to."

"Aww, it's been years since we tried this." He tossed the ball in the air and caught it easily. "You've grown a few inches, plus I know you got your reflexes from me. C'mon now, catch!"

"No!" She put herself between the ball and Wesley, and it bounced off her arm. "I told you, *no*." This was the one thing she would always put her foot down on. Wesley hated sport in general and rugby in particular. She would never force him to play if he didn't want to.

"Whatsamatter?" Chablis asked. Her phone was already raised up, ready to snap a pic. "It's just a ball now, innit? Nothing to be scared of, luv."

"Poppy, stop babying him!" Robbie picked up the ball. "For God's sake, he's old enough to play rugby with his father."

"Not if he doesn't want to."

"Thanks, Mum," Wesley whispered as he grabbed her hand and clung to her side. The anxiety and unease on his face broke her heart, and Poppy knew why: He was scared of disappointing his father again, like he did all those other times when Robbie tried to get him to play.

"C'mon, luv," Chablis called. "Just hold the ball for God's sake! I just need one picture for the press—"

"Shut up, Chablis!" Robbie shouted.

"The *press*?" Poppy's blood pressure shot through the roof. "What do you mean, *press*?"

He shot Chablis a murderous look, then turned to Poppy. "Hey, Pop, it's nothing, okay?"

"Nothing?" The gears in her head turned until everything clicked into place. She knew Robbie too well.

"Mum?" Wesley tugged at her hand.

Taking a deep breath, she reached into her pocket, handed him a fiver, then cocked her head toward the vending machine across the lawn. "Wesley, could you please get me some water?"

He nodded and scampered off.

As soon as he was far enough away, she turned back to Robbie. "Are you using *our child* to get good publicity? Why? You know Wexford's not going to take you back."

His mouth twisted in hate. "I know that," he spat. "No club will, not when they know what I am."

"Then why are you doing this? Why suddenly try to make nice with Wesley in front of the camera, then?"

"You don't understand! After I got kicked out of the league, I lost everything."

"And whose fault was that? I told you not to hide what you were."

"Rugby was—is my life." A vein in his neck throbbed as he gritted his teeth. "I might not be able to play in the Super League again, but I found a way to get everything back."

"Get everything back?"

"Yeah. I'm up to my ears in debt. Bank took my flat, my Porsche, can't even charge anything on my credit card. But I found a way to make money see?" He nodded at Chablis, who, for some reason, was still pointing her camera at them. "A sports apparel company in Australia wants me to be their spokesperson. It's owned by a some big-shot media mogul. He's also talking about starting an all-shifter sports league! They're offering big bucks for me to come over, but I gotta clean up my image first."

"And you thought you'd use *our son* so you can make nice with these people for money?"

"It's not just that." His eyes gleamed. "When they found out I had a son, well they just about went bonkers. They want Wes, too, for their children's line. Think about it—me and him, all over billboards, T-shirts, mugs, stickers! We'll make millions."

Poppy gasped in horror. "I-I'll never allow it!" That would be Wesley's worst nightmare. "He's a minor, and you'll need my consent for that."

His entire face went red, and his hands curled into fists at his side. "Well, I'm his father too."

"Then start acting like it," she hissed. "A real father wouldn't use his son that way."

"I'm doing this for him too! For his future. He'll get loads of money, and he'll never have to work a day in his life ever again."

She screamed in frustration. "If you made even a small effort to get to know him, then you'll realize that's far from what he wants. God!" She threw her hands up. "I can't believe I'm even having this conversation. Goodbye, Robbie!"

"Wait! Poppy! No!" He was suddenly in front of her.

"I'm not letting you go." His tone was deadly, and his eyes glowed inhumanly.

Fear gripped her, and she couldn't speak or breathe.

"If you don't give your consent, then I'll take you to court."

"What?"

"I'll take you to court and ask for full custody."

"You wouldn't dare!"

"Wanna try me, Pop?" he sneered. "He's a shifter cub. I'll find the best lawyer in London who'll argue that he should stay with me because I'll be the only one of us who can raise him right and control him."

"And I'll fight you with everything I've got, just you wait and see!" She was done with this shit. Turning on her heel, she began to walk away, but Robbie grabbed her arm. "Let go of me!"

His grip tightened, then he spun her around. "Stop being difficult! It'll be easier if you just give him to me."

"Never!" she spat. "Ouch! Robbie!" His claws extended out, scraping at her skin.

"Stop!" It was Wesley. He stood a few feet away from them. "Get away from my mum!"

"I—no, Wes!"

But it was too late. Wesley was speeding toward them so fast he was a blur. Robbie's eyes widened, and he raised his other hand, ready to swipe him away.

"No!" She pushed at Robbie with all her might. They tumbled forward, his claws caught on the back of her jumper and ripped through it as he tried to pull away. As she fell to her knees, she yelped in surprise.

From out of nowhere, a loud shriek cut through the air,

drowning her out. The air crackled with energy, and every hair on the back of Poppy's neck rose up. She scrambled to her feet, and when she pushed the tangle of her hair away, she gasped as she saw a tall, imposing figure in all black standing over Robbie.

Rorik.

CHAPTER 9

Control was a big part of Rorik's training growing up. His father drilled the concept into his head, telling him that learning to hold back was just as important as striking out.

But at this very moment, he was about to lose that control.

"You spineless bastard," he spat at the man sprawled on the grass before him. "You dare hurt a woman?"

The man's animal cowered in fear. "I-i-it was an accident, I swear!" He held his hands up to his face. "P-please."

"Rorik ..." Poppy choked out.

Bending down, he grabbed the man—Poppy's ex-husband, he presumed—and hauled him to his feet. "Coward!" His dragon's anger blazed through him like the heat of a thousand suns, urging him to rip the man's throat out. It wanted blood and flesh as payment for the pain he caused their mate.

"P-please!" He choked. "I can't—"

"Rorik, no!" Small hands grabbed at his bicep. "Stop, please, we're in public."

The reminder somehow got through to his brain. *We are guests of this country*, he told his dragon. *We cannot harm any of its citizens.* The dragon hissed at him, but Rorik released the man, anyway. "Swine," he spat, then turned to Poppy. "Are you hurt?"

She shook her head. "No."

He checked her over, searching for blood or wounds through the ripped fabric of her sweater. Though there were no signs of harm, his rage did not abate. Taking his jacket off, he wrapped it around her. "Do you want to call the police? I can also speak to the chief of Buckingham Palace security. The king will want—"

"No, it's—oh, Wesley!" Releasing her death grip on him, she scrambled toward the boy. Or rather, the small cheetah cub who lay on the heap of clothes on the grass a few feet away. Carefully, she lifted him up in her arms. "Oh, Wes. It's all right. Mum's here."

His chest tightened in rage again as he felt the cub's fear and mounting anxiety. His hands curled into fists. "You," he roared at the fiend who hurt Poppy and scared Wesley.

The man in question shot to his feet, brushing the dirt from his clothes. "Who the hell do you think you are? I'm going to report you to—"

Rorik roared again, this time with the force of his dragon. The man promptly clamped his mouth shut and blanched.

"Robbie!" A woman came running up to him. "Robbie, what happened? I kept filming and—"

His expression turned hateful. "Did you hear that, you oaf? I have everything on video. I'm going to make sure you spend the rest of your life in jail for assault!" He turned his malicious gaze to Poppy. "Remember what I said, Pop. I'll have my lawyer contact yours." He spat on the ground, then turned in the opposite direction and walked off.

"Poppy?"

His mate held the cub tighter, her face fraught.

"What can I do, Poppy? Tell me, and I'll do it." *Tell me to rip him to pieces, and I'll do it.*

"I just ... I just want to go back."

"All right. Come, we'll take a taxi back to the palace." He led her out of the park and flagged the first black cab that came by. Opening the door, he let her go inside first, then slid into the seat beside her before telling the driver their destination. "Is he all right?" he whispered, glancing down at her lap.

She had Wesley wrapped up in his clothes so the driver wouldn't see him. "Yes. He's sleeping. Excitement makes him tired."

"Ah."

"Rorik?"

"Yes?"

"What are you doing here?"

"Um ..."

"Were you following us?"

"Er, yes." He could not lie to her now, not even if he wanted to. "I'm sorry. This is a violation of your privacy. But I had a terrible feeling. See ... Gideon told me you had left to meet your ex-husband." That information already sent him into a jealous rage, but what the other dragon had told him made him even more furious. "He said ... Wesley told him he didn't want to see his father."

She went pale. "I wasn't forcing him, if that's what you

think. I have to abide by our custody agreement that says they have to meet whenever Wes is in London. He's still Wes's father. He's never hurt Wes, and—"

"Poppy." He placed a hand on her arm. "Please do not think I am accusing you of anything or this is your fault." No, it was that bastard's fault. "Anyway, I just ... wanted to make sure you and Wesley were all right. I Cloaked myself and shifted, then flew to this park. I had no plans of interfering until I saw you argue and he ..." It was difficult to continue. When Robbie put his hands on her, he lost his temper, and he swooped down to stop him. "You are probably angry with me for following you here. I was just ... following a gut feeling."

"You were right then." She slumped back into the seat. "He didn't hurt us. Not physically, anyway. But you see, Robbie, he ... all he wanted was a son who was just like him. Athletic, outgoing. He tried, he really did, but he got so frustrated because all Wes wanted to do was read and study. I did my best to protect Wes. I never talked badly about Robbie in front of him.

"When the scandal broke out, I was hounded by the press for interviews, offered amounts that made my head spin, but I didn't accept them, not even when we were nearly homeless. I couldn't have him read those things one day and realize what a terrible man his father was. And I just thought that Robbie would magically change the more he spent time with Wes. I'm a horrible mum, allowing him to keep on hurting Wes like that." She closed her eyes, but he could see the glitter of tears trapped between her lashes.

"You are a good mother, do not doubt that." And he knew that from the beginning. He saw it from how she protected Wesley. He heard it when she counseled the queen when she was worried about being a parent. And from the night of the party, when she told him how she sacrificed everything for Wesley. Though her rejection had crushed his soul and his dragon, she nonetheless earned his respect.

"Oh God! Robbie!" She sat up quickly, then shrank back when Wes let out a protesting cry, but his eyes remained shut. "Sorry," she soothed. "I'm sorry, Wes. Don't worry, I won't let your dad take you away from me."

"Take him away? What are you talking about?"

She swallowed audibly, then looked up at him. "Robbie ... he wants to fight for custody." Taking a deep breath, she told him what had transpired before Rorik had arrived. "... and so, he says he's going to take me to court. They might rule in his favor because he's a shifter."

The rage he thought had long gone was now seeping back into him. "That son of a—" He ground his teeth together. "Do not worry, Poppy. I will take care of it."

"Take care of it?" she asked, puzzled. "How?"

He wasn't sure how, exactly, but he would find a way.

The cab slowed to a stop. "Come, let's get you both inside."

"Are we allowed to just walk in?" Poppy asked as they alighted from the vehicle. "What about Wes? What if they see him? Or he wakes up and shifts back?"

As captain of the Dragon Guard, it would be easy for him to go in and flash his security badge, but Poppy was right. He would have to sneak them in. "I will Cloak us and get us past the guards."

"Cloak ... that invisibility thing you do?"

"Yes. Now," he wrapped an arm around her shoulder. "As long as we are touching and you have Wesley in your arms, you shall be Cloaked as well. Do not let go of me or make a sound."

"A-all right."

With a deep breath, he called on his abilities, feeling it settle around them. He squeezed her shoulder and led her around to the back of the palace. He slowed down when he saw a car approach the security gate, then deftly steered them to walk at pace behind the vehicle to get past the guards. From there, it was much easier, and soon he delivered them safely to their room.

"Stay in here and get some rest," he said as she opened the door. "Let me know if Wesley requires medical attention."

"The prince—"

"Is fine. He is with Ingrid." he said. "I will make sure she stays with him for the rest of the day. You must rest."

"But—"

"Rest." On impulse, he pressed a kiss to her temple. He heard her gasp—a pleasant sound that sent a soothing warmth to his very bones. "Trust me, I will take care of everything."

"T-thank you, Rorik," she whispered as she stepped into the room. Turning around, she looked up at him, those obsidian eyes filled with gratitude. "Thank you for everything."

He could not move or breathe, not until the door closed. Being so close to her, smelling her sweet scent and feeling her skin against his lips had taken the air from his lungs. He wanted to savor the moment as it might be the last time he would ever be so close to her. His dragon hung its head limply.

I cannot wallow in misery forever. For now, he would

distract himself as there was so much to be done. He headed down the hall toward the library that had been turned into the Northern Isles delegation's office. It was empty, thankfully, as the queen and king were still out and about.

He sat down at one of the desks, trying to figure out what to do. First, he had to see to Poppy and Wesley. So, he picked up the phone and called the butler assigned to them.

"This is Smith. To whom I am speaking?" said the crisp, posh voice on the other line.

"I am Rorik, captain of the Dragon Guard of the Northern Isles."

"Good evening, captain, how may I be of service?"

"Could you please send over some tea and a tray of food to Ms. Baxter's room please?"

"Of course, I'll get on it right away. Is there anything else?"

"No—yes." He recalled how frightened Wesley had been. "Would it be possible to borrow a few books from the library? It's for Wesley, Ms. Baxter's son. Or you may send someone to the nearest bookstore and charge it to our accounts."

"I'll see to it, but if I may ask, what kind of books would you like?"

"I ... uh ..." He scratched his head. Wesley did mention that one book that first time he'd seen him in the library at Helgeskar Palace. "How about *The Hobbit*? Or anything by the same author?"

"Ah, yes, we have copies of those in the library. I'll send them along."

"Thank you, Smith." He hung up. Next, he had to contact Gideon. He was overseeing the security for the day's activities, which thankfully occurred just within the walls of Buckingham Palace, so he sent him a text message.

Call me back as soon as possible.

The reply came in seconds. *Tea with the queen just finished. See you in a few.*

As he waited for Gideon to arrive, Rorik got to his feet and paced around the room, trying to expend the pent-up anger and frustration he'd been keeping in check. *I have to find a way to stop her ex-husband from gaining custody of Wesley.* But how? He didn't even know the first thing about how human courts worked.

"What's wrong?" Gideon asked as soon as he came through the door. "Is it Poppy? Wesley? Where are they?"

"They're back in their room," he said, then relayed what had happened.

"Mother Frigga!" He must have been really angry because he almost never cursed. "They're all right, though?"

"I think so." He leaned back in the leather chair. "I want him gone from their lives. Obliterated."

"Me too, but you can't do anything rash now." Gideon walked over to the couch and sat down. "We need to think logically about this."

"He said he would take her to court. What would happen then?"

"Well, I imagine England has some kind of family court system. She needs a lawyer to represent her if Robbie does sue for custody."

"Then let's find the best one for her. I don't care how much it costs or what it takes." He hardly touched his salary from his job, plus, his personal trust fund from his family was more than he could spend in this lifetime. "But how can we make sure he does not win?"

"Hmmm ... you said there was someone taking a video of the entire thing?"

"That's what Poppy said."

Gideon smiled, and a twinkle in his eyes appeared. "Leave it to me then. I have an idea."

CHAPTER 10

As soon as the door to their room shut behind them, Poppy strode to the bed, scrambled on top, and laid Wesley on the mattress, "Oh, Wes," she cried. "I'm sorry. I'm so sorry." She buried her face in her hands. *I shouldn't have agreed to this.* The moment she saw Robbie acting strange, she should have taken Wes away. This was all her fault.

"Mum?"

Wiping her tears away, she put her hands to her lap. "Wes! Are you all right?"

He let out a long yawn. "Just tired."

"Are you hurt? Did he—"

"No, Mum. I shifted into my cheetah, and I tried to get to you, then Rorik ... his dragon came. I couldn't see him at first, but I knew he was there. It's so big and ... scary."

"Oh, Wes." She pulled him into her arms and pressed her nose into his hair. He was scared of Rorik. How did she not see that? "This is all my fault. I'm sorry. Sorry Rorik scared you. And sorry about your dad."

He sniffed. "It's not your fault, Mum. It's mine. I should have tried harder, like Dad said. That way, he—"

"No, no!" She held him tighter. "You're wonderful as you are, Wes. Don't ever, ever change. I'm sorry if you ever felt you had to for him and if I didn't tell you that you are enough as you are."

"Did he ... did Dad hurt you?"

"No, Wes. I'm fine." She gulped.

"Rorik ... he came in time?"

"Yes, I guess Rorik did." She wasn't sure what he meant by 'in time'. Would Robbie have seriously hurt them? Before, she wouldn't have thought him capable. But now that he had lost everything he cared about, she wasn't sure.

"I'm glad Rorik showed up, Mum. I thought he was ... that he was like ..."

"Like what?"

"Nothing." He slumped against her. "Is Dad going to take me away? So I can pose for pictures with him?"

"What? How did you—"

"I wasn't fully asleep. I ... heard you and Rorik talking in the car."

Oh, Wes. "Don't you worry about that. I won't let him take you." A knock on the door interrupted her. "Wait here, okay?" Scrambling off the bed, she walked over to the door and opened it. "Yes?"

"Good evening." A young man stood on the other side. "I have tea for you, Miss Baxter. And some books." He held up the tray in his hand.

"Tea ... and books? From whom? I didn't order anything."

"I don't know, ma'am. Should I take these back, then?"

"I—"

"Books?" Wesley called from the bed. "What books?"

"I believe it's *The Hobbit* and *The Lord of the Rings* trilogy," the young man said. "They're from the palace library. I was told they were to be lent to Master Wesley."

"Tolkien?" Wesley raced to the door. "Really? Mum, can I read them?"

"Uh, I suppose that's fine. Thank you, uh …"

"Mercer, ma'am," the young man said as he walked into the room and placed the tray on the table. "If you need anything else, just ring us."

"Thank you, Mercer." She walked him to the door, then closed it when he stepped out.

"Mum, I think these are first edition!" Wesley exclaimed as he ran a hand over the leather-bound books reverently.

The way his face lit up made her heart soar. Who could have sent them tea and books?

Well, who else knows you're back?

Rorik.

Could it be … but then her inner voice was right. He was the only one who knew they were back early. He also came to them and watched over them because he was worried about Robbie. *Oh dear, he could have gotten into trouble, leaving the king and queen.*

The tea and books were such a kind and sweet gesture, her insides were now practically melting. She could almost forget all the troubles from today. Maybe that wouldn't be so bad right now. She would worry about Robbie and the upcoming custody battle later. Seeing her son happy at this moment was a victory she would cherish, even if it did come as a surprise and from the most unexpected source.

When she thought she couldn't have been more surprised, the call she got the next morning utterly floored her.

"Hello?" She had picked up the phone without looking at it because they were getting ready to leave the palace for the airport.

"Is this Ms. Poppy Baxter?"

"Yes, this is she. How—hold on!" Placing the phone down, she picked up a bundle of clothing and placed them in her suitcase, then called to Wesley, who was still in the bathroom. "Hurry up, Wes! We're leaving in ten minutes. If you're not out of there, we're going to France without you!" Picking the phone back up, she put it to her ear. "Sorry. Um, who is this?"

"My name is Ian Grayford. I'm a solicitor with Irvine Prescott International."

A solicitor? "What can I do for you, Mr. Grayford?"

"Well, Ms. Baxter, my firm has been hired to defend you regarding a possible custody battle with your ex-husband."

She froze in the act of closing her suitcase lid as his words computed. "Hired? But I didn't hire you or your firm, Mr. Grayford."

"Nonetheless, my services have been acquired on your behalf, and I'm already preparing to meet with your ex-husband's lawyers proactively."

"Can I afford you? I don't have a lot of money." The last solicitor she used when she and Robbie divorced had cost her a pretty penny, and while she already had most of her salary saved from the last month, she was hoping to put that toward Wesley's school fees.

"The retainer has been paid, Ms. Baxter. In advance."

"But who did? You have to tell me who's paying for you, don't you?"

"Hold on, let me check my email ... ah. It seems the request came from the biggest client of our legal finance department. Aumont Industries."

Aumont? *Gideon!* It had to be him. Oh Lord, Gideon hired a solicitor for her? But why?

"Ms. Baxter?"

"Uh, yes?" She checked the time. Ten more minutes. "I'm sorry ... I'm kind of in a rush here as I'm on my way to the airport. But ... do you think I have a chance of fighting this?"

"I can assure you I will do my very best, Ms. Baxter. But I can tell you that I take on cases like this all the time, and we can discuss strategies. How about I call you again later?"

"Sure. Tonight would be good. I'll be free around seven. Thank you so much, Mr. Grayford."

"Of course, Ms. Baxter. I'll talk to you later."

Her hands shook as she put the phone down. It was difficult to contain her excitement and relief, and tears sprang at the corner of her eyes. Mr. Grayford sounded competent, and for the first time since yesterday, she wasn't worried about losing Wesley. Still, there was a battle ahead, but at least having a solicitor in London took a big load off her shoulders.

"Oh, Gideon!" She had to thank him and offer to pay off the legal fees. Yikes. Would she be able to afford it? Maybe she could pay in installments every month or something. In any case, she'd have to talk to him. And of course, Rorik as well. He must have mentioned her legal troubles to Gideon. *Yes, I'll have to thank them both.*

However, with the tight schedule for the rest of the week

—two days in Cannes before heading to Paris—she didn't see either of the two except for when they were on the plane, and there was hardly any privacy there.

Finally, it was at the end of the week when Wesley was headed back to the Northern Isles when she had a chance to see Gideon. She went down to the hotel lobby to see him off when she spotted the Dragon Guard waiting by the concierge desk.

"Hey, Poppy, Wes," he greeted. "Are you ready for our trip back?"

"Yup!" he said.

"I'll take good care of him," Gideon promised.

"I know you will. Wes, could you give me and Gideon a moment? I need to speak with him. Why don't you go to the bathroom before you leave for the airport? It's a long trip."

"Sure, Mum." He dashed over in the direction of the restrooms.

Gideon cocked his head. "Poppy? What is it?"

"I wanted to thank you for getting that solicitor to take on my case," she began.

"Oh that? That was no trouble at all. I'm only glad my family connections have finally been useful to someone."

"You don't know what it means to me. Mr. Grayford's been so helpful, and he promised to take care of everything, I don't even have to show up in person. Not having to worry about court dates and filings is a big relief. Thank you."

"You're very welcome, Poppy. Wes is a wonderful kid, and you're a great mom. And I would hate to lose my favorite library buddy," he laughed.

"You'll have to let me pay you back somehow."

"What? Oh. No, Poppy." He held up a hand. "You don't owe me anything."

"But I do. I can imagine Mr. Grayford's firm must charge a lot by the hour, and I'm sure we can work out—"

"No, I mean, you really don't owe *me* anything. I just called the firm and threw my name around. But I didn't pay for anything."

"You didn't?" Now she was confused. "Then who did?"

"Rorik did. In fact, it was his idea to hire a solicitor for you."

Her jaw dropped. "It was?"

"Yes. Believe me, this was all his doing."

"All of it?"

"Yeah. He even gave me the idea for—" He stopped short.

"Idea for what?"

There was a strange look in his eyes. "Let's just say ... you probably won't have to worry about your ex gaining custody of Wesley. You might find he won't even try to sue for custody at all."

"What? But how?"

"Oh, there's our driver." He waved toward the direction of the doors. "We really should get going. I'll let you have a few moments alone with Wesley and meet you outside."

"Sure." Her mind, though, still reeled from the new information. It was Rorik. It was all Rorik. He came to them that day and took them away. Sent them tea and books for Wesley to comfort him. And then he paid for a solicitor to defend her against Robbie.

"Mum?" Wesley tugged at her skirt.

"Yes?" She didn't even notice he had come back. "Uh, are you ready?"

"I am."

Walking hand in hand, they left the lobby and stepped onto the driveway. "Oh dear," she began as she saw the door of the limo open. "I can't believe ... I mean, this is this longest I'll be away from you since ... well, since you were born." She held her tears in check, not wanting to embarrass Wes in front of Gideon.

"I'll be fine, Mum," he groaned, rolling his eyes. "Really, I will. School will keep me busy, and before you know it, you'll be back."

She gave him a weak smile. "You're right, I'm being silly." At least he was back to normal. She fretted, thinking he'd been scarred by the incident at the park. *I need to have faith in Wesley and his resilience.* Bending down to his level, she gave him a hug. "Be good, all right? And if you need anything call me anytime, day or night. Or ask Gideon."

"All right." His lips pursed together. "Mum?"

"Yes?"

"Could you ... could you tell Rorik I said thank you? When I returned the books to the butler, he told me that Rorik had requested them for me."

"Really?"

"Yeah, and ... I think ..." He swallowed audibly. "I was wrong about him."

"Wrong? How?"

"I thought he was scary, and my cheetah and I were both frightened of him. He was big and tall, and his dragon was so fierce. But then he came to help us, and ... well, if you wanted to be his friend, I'd be okay with it now."

"Oh, Wes." She pulled him in for another hug.

"So, *are* you going to be friends with him?"

Was he asking what she thought he was asking? He probably was, the little smarty-pants. But all she could do was chuckle. "We'll see."

"I wouldn't mind if you did."

"Wes," Gideon called from inside the car. "Time to leave."

With one last hug, she let him go. "Love you, Wes."

"Love you too, Mum!" He waved at her, then the door shut.

Pushing herself up, she watched the limo drive away. *He'll be fine*, she told herself. Besides, if she was acting like a scared mother hen just being separated from him for a week, what would she do when he was gone for months at boarding school?

The blast of chilly air reminded her that it was time to head inside. She should have taken her coat along and gone for a walk. It was Sunday night, and Queen Sybil had insisted that everyone—including herself and the king—take the afternoon and evening off, and thus there were no events scheduled. *Maybe I should go out.* She'd only been to Paris once, on a school trip when she was a teenager. Besides, when else was she going to get to see the most romantic city in the world?

She headed back up to the top floor where the Northern Isles delegation had taken up the presidential suite and all the rooms surrounding it. Her room was near the end because the rooms right next to the suites were taken up by Gideon and—

Rorik.

She stopped in the middle of the hallway. *I should go say thank you.* It would be polite. And she had to convince him to at least let her pay him back, even if it took her years. Yes, it was the right thing to do.

Spinning on her heel, she marched up to the door next to the suite. She gave it three strong raps and waited. Seconds ticked by and ... nothing.

Maybe he wasn't in his room?

Oh God, what if he was busy? What if he wasn't alone? *I should go.*

Suddenly, the door flung open. "Poppy?"

"Rorik, I—" *Oh Lord.*

He was there all right, standing in the doorway, wearing nothing but a towel around his waist, showing off his perfectly formed eight pack. Droplets of water clung to his hair, beard, and the expanse of his wide, muscled, tattooed chest. Her pulse went mad, and heat coiled in her belly. She felt like one of those old-school cartoons where the wolf's eyes popped out of their sockets when an attractive woman walked by. "Uh, h-hey, Rorik."

His brows furrowed as he gestured for her to come in. "Is everything all right?" he asked, leaning forward just for a second to reach behind her and shut the door. "Is something wrong? Is it Wesley?"

"Who—oh right." She forced herself to lift her gaze away from his muscled torso. "I spoke to Gideon before he left. He said you were the one who paid for the solicitor to help us."

He sucked in a breath and rubbed the back of his head. "I ... yes. I hope you did not think I was overstepping my bounds. It was an opportunity to help you, so I did it."

"Thank you, Rorik." Her heart thudded loudly now. "You didn't have to do that for me or Wes. Not any of it—not even sending those books for him or watching over us at the park."

"Of course I did."

"Why?" It was the burning question in her head. "Why go through all that trouble for us? What do you care if I lose custody of Wesley or not?"

"Because he is your world, your happiness," he stated. "And I could not bear it if you lost him and have you unhappy."

The words struck her like lightning hitting a tree—a bright flash that seared her insides and ignited something in her. She wasn't sure what exactly, but before she knew it, she launched herself at him, pulling him down to press her lips to his.

His entire body stiffened for a split second, but then he began to kiss her back. Strong arms wound around her, and a hand wrapped around the nape of her neck, massaging her until she opened her mouth, and his tongue snaked in to tease and taste her.

Her body's temperature shot up, and her hands roamed his naked chest, caressing the warm skin and the hard muscles. She slipped her arms behind him and raked her fingers down his back, digging her nails gently into him. That move earned her a growl, and she found herself being lifted up. It took only three strides before he deposited her on top of his bed.

She crawled back on her elbows, wanting to look at him. He stood over her, the towel still somehow magically clinging to his trim waist. Her heart thudded as his hands moved down to loosen it and let it drop to the floor.

Oh Lord, he was magnificent. Her mouth watered at the perfect abs and deep V of his hips that led her gaze lower to his fully erect cock. Her clit practically throbbed at the sight of it.

The mattress dipped as he climbed on the bed and moved closer to her, his large frame covering hers as she lay on her back. His weight pressed down deliciously on her as he lowered himself, his head coming down to hers to kiss her again. His lips were surprisingly gentle this time as if savoring her. She arched up against him, wanting more, and as if sensing her need, his hand slipped under her top, then lifted the hem up and over her head before tossing it aside.

His eyes glittered like emeralds as he stared down at her, devouring her with his gaze. Large hands reached to cup her breasts, pulling the cups down to expose her nipples. She moaned and closed her eyes as he teased them into buds, rolling them between his fingers.

Something wet and warm closed over her left nipple, and her eyes shot open. His head was bent down, mouth on her breast. His tongue lashed against the pointed bud while his hand continued to tweak the other. She squirmed under his touch, pushing her hips up at him and his erection pressed against her thighs.

He lifted her skirt higher and moved a hand between her legs. His fingers skimmed along her panties, teasing her through the now damp fabric.

"Rorik ... oh, please ..."

He responded by pulling her panties down, and she lifted her hips to get them off. A finger slid up and down her slit, making her even wetter. He dipped one finger inside, then found her clit and teased her button until she was panting and squirming.

He released her nipple and began to trail kisses down her

stomach. Flipping her skirt over, he positioned his head between her thighs, his mouth and teeth nipping and sucking all the way down to her apex.

A cry escaped her mouth when he replaced his fingers with his mouth. His lips teased her clit, his tongue lapping up her juices. She couldn't stop herself even if she wanted to as her body shuddered in orgasm.

"Yes," he moaned. "Beautiful."

Her breath came in pants as she practically melted into the mattress. He moved between her thighs again, then reached for something on the bedside table, taking out a foil wrapped condom.

Leave it to the French to have that as part of their amenities, she thought wryly.

He ripped the packet open with his teeth, then slipped the condom on. Bracing himself on one elbow, he covered her body. Her arms slipped around his shoulders as she felt the tip of his cock nudge at her and then began to slide inside her.

She braced herself for him, holding her breath as she accommodated his length and girth. His fingers found their way to her clit again, teasing the bud until she grew wetter with each inch he slipped in her. She nudged up at him, letting him know she needed him to move.

And he did. Slow at first, long languid strokes that sent little whorls of heat through her, before igniting like wildfire. His hands roamed all over, branding her as his fingers trailed across her skin. Her body tightened and wanted more though, but he continued to take his time. Unable to stop herself, she raked her nails down his shoulder and arms.

"Faster," she urged. "Harder, please, Rorik. I need more."

He groaned, but then obliged, building up a steady

rhythm. Grabbing her knees, he pushed them up, and pushed deeper into her, hitting just the right spot over and over again that sent her over the edge. Her body was barely recovering when he pulled out, then flipped her onto her stomach. Hauling her hips to him, he thrust hard into her, his hand slipping underneath her to pluck at her clit. His primal grunts became louder, his thrusts harder, and before she knew it, she was coming again. His body shuddered, then his movements became erratic. Fingers dug into her hips, and he gave one last thrust and let out a guttural cry as his cock twitched inside her.

She slumped forward, feeling boneless. She sighed as Rorik withdrew, then rolled off her, landing beside her. Her limbs felt like jelly, and she didn't want to move. Couldn't move, really. The orgasms he had wrung from her left her weak.

They both lay in silence for a few minutes before she could make her vocal cords work again. "That was ..."

"Magnificent," he finished, scooping an arm under her to pull her on top of him.

She squealed but settled against his chest, placing her chin in her hands so she could look up at him. Those green eyes twinkled, making him look even more handsome. His hand reached down and brushed her hair away from her face. She closed her eyes and rubbed her cheek against his warm palm. The sex had been phenomenal, but what was more amazing was that she didn't feel awkward right now. This all just felt so ... right.

"I like seeing you like this."

"Like what?"

"I like seeing you smile," he said. "Especially when you smile just for me."

Heat bloomed in her cheeks. "Thank you. You're not bad yourself. Hey!" She let out a shriek when he suddenly rolled them over so he pinned her to mattress.

"So lovely," he whispered against her neck. "I could stay with you like this forever."

Oh, so could she. Especially when he nuzzled her neck so deliciously. However, there was another need she couldn't quite ignore—her stomach. "Rorik ..."

"Hmmm?"

"I'm hungry. I haven't had a chance to eat because I was getting Wes packed up. Do you think we can go outside and get something to eat?"

He stopped and propped himself up on his elbows. "Outside?"

"Yeah ... like dinner. Oh—" She clamped her lips shut. "I mean, it wouldn't be like a date or anything."

"No! I mean, yes ... of course it would be a date."

"R-really?"

"Definitely." He frowned. "However, I cannot leave the hotel, not when the king and queen are here. I was only able to come to the park with you yesterday because Gideon covered for me. But Niklas only arrived this afternoon and has not been briefed."

"Oh. Right." She couldn't help feeling disappointed. "I guess I could go by myself."

"By yourself? No, that's not—hold on, I have an idea." He rolled off her.

She couldn't help but watch his naked, glorious body on display as he slid off the bed and stretched out.

He picked up the discarded towel from the floor and wrapped it around his waist. "Come," he said, offering her his hand.

Taking it, she found herself pulled out of bed. He grabbed a robe hanging from the headboard, wrapped it around her, then led her out to the balcony. "Where are we—oh!" Outside, there was a magnificent view of the famous Paris rooftops and the Eiffel Tower. "Wow, this is amazing."

"It is," he said, his voice soft and eyes never leaving hers. "I shall call for room service, and we can eat out here." He gestured to the table and chairs set up on the deck. "Will this be a satisfactory first date?"

"Oh, yes," she sighed, then snuggled to his side. "Very satisfactory."

CHAPTER 11

Well, well now, Niklas remarked through their mental link as he strode into the presidential suite's main living room for the morning briefing. *Don't you look chipper this morning?*

Rorik picked up his cup of coffee and took a sip. *I beg your pardon?*

You're smiling, Niklas pointed out. *You don't always smile this early. At least not like that.*

I don't know what you mean.

The other dragon crossed the room and stood over him. *Dude, c'mon. I'm right next to you. I could hear you two. Both times.*

Rorik promptly spit out the coffee. "Gods ... I ..."

Niklas roared with laughter. "Holy shit, I wish I had my phone out to take a picture!" Plopping down on the couch, he slapped Rorik on the back. "Hey, it's cool."

"We should have been more discreet." He wiped his mouth and the table with a napkin. "Apologies for the disturbance."

"I went to university in America, I'm used to it." Niklas grabbed a piece of toast from the tray and took a bite. "I'm just glad you finally made your move and got out of the friend zone. High five!"

Rorik glared at him, not wanting to encourage such talk about his mate. His dragon, however, let out a smug snort of satisfaction. Then again, he felt the same.

Being with Poppy was one of the most satisfying and intense experiences of his life. They made love again after dinner, but unfortunately, she had to sneak back to her room afterwards as she wanted some sleep before getting up early the next day. He didn't want her to go, but he, too, had his duties. Though the queen had declared Sunday as a rest day for the staff, there was no such thing for him. He had to stay alert at all times. In fact, even during his off-hours, he only slept an hour or two before leaving his room to patrol the halls or the perimeter of their designated hotel.

"So, what are you gonna do now?" Niklas finished the toast and wiped his mouth with a napkin. "Are you bonded yet?"

"No, not yet." It was said that bonding with a mate was a special event and that one would know if it happened. But, both of them had to be open to forming the bond. "She doesn't know about us being mates."

"She doesn't? Why haven't you told her?"

"I ... I'm not sure how." Many, many times last night he wanted to tell her. He nearly did blurt it out at certain points, desperate as he was to claim her. Yet there was also fear lurking about. Fear that she wouldn't understand, or worse, would be scared of the bond. Her ex-husband had been a shifter and treated her badly, after all.

Niklas tsked. "Well, she's not gonna find out any other way unless you do."

"I know I should, but ... it's just complicated at the moment. With the tour. It would be different if we were back home, but out here, the king and queen are exposed. They need my full attention. Perhaps when we head back—"

"That might be too late! And then Wesley will be there. I think it's fairly obvious he's not a fan of yours."

Yes, there was that. She loved her son more than anything in the world. At first, he thought he and his dragon would be jealous that Wesley would always be her top priority, but surprisingly, he respected her even more for it.

But the boy was wary of Rorik; Anyone would have felt Wesley's anxiety and panic whenever Rorik came near. He guessed that that first meeting when he swooped down to attack the child did him no favors. Somehow, he would have to win him over as well.

"I like Wesley, he's a great kid. But this could be your only chance to tell her she's your fated mate. Because the bond can't possibly form if you keep this from her, right? You have to spend as much time as you can with her, and I'm not just talking about in the bedroom. Go and have a romantic dinner. Take her somewhere special. Then tell her how you feel."

"How I feel?"

"Don't tell me you're not in love with her yet. That grin on your face this morning told me so."

Oh, Yggdrasil.

He was in love with Poppy.

His dragon heartily cheered him on.

But to tell her was another matter. As a human, she

might think it was too soon. "When am I supposed to tell her? This week is even busier than that last." In the next seven days, they would be zipping through four more cities —Barcelona, Madrid, Rome—and then end the tour in Venice.

Niklas let out an exasperated sigh. "Why don't you just give me more hours? And delegate more tasks to the private security firm we hired? That's what they're there for, right? Take a couple hours tonight when she's done working."

The temptation to say yes and throw caution to the wind lurked in his mind. But he was captain of the Dragon Guard. "No, I cannot. My duty is to my king and queen." And that came first. He could not just abandon his post.

"Dude—"

"Rorik, Niklas," King Aleksei greeted as he walked into the living room. Queen Sybil came up behind him, then Poppy followed, carrying Prince Alric. When their eyes met, Rorik could feel his stomach churn with excitement and desire, and from the way her eyes sparkled before she turned away, she felt the same way.

He longed for her, to tell her that he loved her, but he wanted to wait for the right moment. Last night when she left, they hadn't exactly made plans to see each other again, and he wasn't sure when they would next be alone.

"Rorik?"

Niklas kicked him in the shin.

"Er, yes Your Majesty?"

King Aleksei narrowed his eyes at him. "Are you all right?"

"Yes, I'm fine. I just ... I was about to brief Niklas on this week's schedule." Picking up the tablet computer from the table, he turned the screen on. "Let's begin, shall we? On today's agenda...."

While he was able to concentrate on the briefing, he tracked Poppy's presence in the background as she fed the prince his breakfast. How he longed to go to her now, but his duty came first.

When their meeting wound down and King Aleksei dismissed them, he caught Poppy's gaze as she sat on the carpet with the prince. She smiled up shyly at him, and he gave her a small nod. Later, he thought. He would go to her, and they could talk.

However, it seemed time deliberately slowed down to spite him. The day felt endless, especially since they were traveling again. By the time he finished ensuring the security of the king and queen's new suite, the grandfather clock in the living room struck midnight. Would Poppy still be awake at this time? He didn't want to disturb her sleep, but he needed to see her, and so his dragon urged him to go to her room.

When he stood outside her door, he raised his hand to knock, but it flew open.

"Rorik." She didn't look like she had been sleeping. In fact, she looked positively gorgeous, dressed in a sexy low-cut red dress that showed off a generous amount of cleavage and set her coppery skin all aglow. She wore a hint of makeup, just enough to enhance her already perfect features, while her springy curly hair hung loose around her.

"Poppy ... you—" Before he could finish, she grabbed him by the collar and pulled him inside. When the door closed, she pushed him up against it and plastered her body to his. "I'm afraid I don't have a lot of time."

"That's all right." She reached down to his belt. "I'll take whatever you can give me."

Oh, Yggdrasil.

He helped her unbuckle the belt and take out his cock, which was already rock hard. Her hand wrapped around him, squeezing and stroking him in a way that made him thrust his hips into her fingers. The pleasure built up until it became too much. With a growl, he flipped their positions, then lifted her up against the wall. He reached into his pocket and took out the condom he had put in there earlier, then ripped the packet apart and slipped the rubber on.

"I need you, Rorik," she moaned, her dark pupils blowing up. "Please."

He pulled her dress up, intending to take her underwear off but was pleasantly surprised to find out she was wearing none. *Minx.* He teased her with his fingers until he was sure she was wet enough to accommodate him, then slipped his hands under her thighs to impale her on him. She cried out, and her arms clung to him as he thrust into her, the feeling of her gripping his cock and sliding in and out of her frazzling his brain until he couldn't think of anything but pleasure.

"I'm coming, oh God, Rorik."

He didn't stop until her body tightened around him. As she came down from her orgasm, he managed to walk them over to the bed. He sat down, letting her knees rest on the mattress as she slipped her dress over her head. She grabbed onto his shoulders and began to move.

Lying back, he watched her as she rode him, her breasts bouncing with each thrust, head thrown back as she moaned and continued to take her pleasure. She squeezed him hard, gripping his cock with each downward motion. The friction of her made his eyes roll back, and when her body shuddered, he lost his control. He grabbed her thighs and thrust up into her, his cock pulsing as he came and filled up the condom before he collapsed back down.

"Wow ..." He stared up at the ceiling, trying to find his words. "That was ... surprising."

She laughed, then moved her hips until he slipped out of her. However, she remained in position, straddling him. "You can't come to me looking like that and not expect me to keep my hands to myself."

"Like what?"

"So ... yummy in this suit." Her hands trailed down his shirt, wrapped his tie around her fingers, then gave it a tug and—holy Mother Frigga—the tension caused his cock to stir again.

"Poppy," he warned as she looked down seductively at him, twirling the silk between her fingers.

"How much time do you have left?"

He glanced at the clock and cursed silently. Rolling her underneath him, he pinned her to the mattress, then pushed her thighs apart. "Do not worry, we will make the most of it." There was just not enough time to do everything he wanted or say what needed to be said. Maybe tomorrow.

CHAPTER 12

Poppy couldn't help the disappointment settling over her as she reached over to the other side of the bed and felt cool sheets. Once again, Rorik had gone back to his duty of guarding the king and queen. The captain of the Dragon Guard kept no regular hours, after all, not out here where there could be danger about. And she understood, she truly did. But that didn't mean she had to like it.

It's not that he left her unsatisfied. The sex was out of this world. No one from her past could compare to Rorik. All he had to do was look at her, and she burst into flames.

Though they couldn't socialize during the day, nevertheless, Rorik acknowledged her in small ways. If he was waiting by the door, he would send her a knowing glance, the corners of his mouth twitching. Or if they were at some event, he would casually brush against her as he passed by. It was exciting but also nerve-racking, and made her anticipate what was to come. Every night when he managed to escape for an hour or two, he snuck into her room. Their time together was brief, but they made the most of it.

Beep. Beep. Beep.

The alarm on her phone reminded her that she needed to get up, and with a deep stretch, she got out of bed and prepared for the day. They had arrived in Venice from Rome last night, and they would spend two nights here before going back home. Poppy had to dress properly today as she and Prince Alric would be joining the king and queen for a tour along the canals, so she put on a turtleneck sweater, a wool skirt, and slipped on a pair of knee-high boots over her thick tights.

"Good morning, Poppy," the queen greeted as Poppy entered their suite. She nodded at Prince Alric, who sat in his high chair. "I've prepared his food. You just need to feed him while I get dressed. Could you please be ready to leave by nine o'clock?"

"Of course, Your Majesty."

The day stretched on, and though Poppy enjoyed the tour and seeing the canals and famous sights of Venice, all she could think about was tonight.

She did her job, made sure the prince was taken care of throughout the day, and when Ingrid came to take over, she went back to her room to video chat with Wes. She missed him of course, but he seemed to be doing well; thriving actually. She almost wanted to cry by the time they said goodbye because she realized that he was growing up so fast, and soon they would be separated for longer periods of time once he went to boarding school.

Of course, thinking about Wes made her wonder about what his reaction to Rorik would be. Though he'd mentioned that he was all right with Rorik and Poppy being "friends," what about if they became romantically involved?

She'd never introduced him to any boyfriend as there had been no time for anything more than a few flings after the divorce.

Maybe I don't even have to worry until we get back to the Northern Isles. Assuming they would continue ... whatever this was they were doing. There hadn't been time to talk about what this was exactly, but she wanted more. Would he feel the same? What about their jobs, his duty to the king? How would it affect them?

After a long, hot shower, she went to bed, curling up with a book to pass the time. Her body practically buzzed with anticipation as she waited for midnight, and sure enough, the knock came. She flew to the door and opened it to let Rorik in.

"Poppy—"

She wasted no time and pulled him inside, kissing him full on the mouth. The thrill of that first touch was like a drug she couldn't get enough of. They were tearing each other's clothes, and they didn't even make it to bed and ended up making love on the floor.

"Oh my," she giggled as he pulled out and rolled over onto the plush carpet next to her.

"I'm sorry ... I needed you so bad," he said.

"It's all right. Did you eat at all? Or sleep?"

"I do not need as much sleep as humans." He propped himself up on his side. "And how about you? Are you getting enough rest? I cannot forgive myself if I am making you too exhausted to perform your duties."

"Don't worry about me." She let out a deep sigh.

"How can I not?" He reached over and brushed her hair away from her face, his fingers caressing her cheek. "You seem glum tonight. Is something the matter? Have I done anything to offend you?"

"What? Oh ... no."

"Please, Poppy, tell me. Tell me, and I will make everything better."

"You say the sweetest things." She nuzzled at his palm. "Rorik, is this real? What we're doing?"

"Real?"

Though her heart pounded in her chest and her stomach churned in discomfort, she had to know. There was so much at stake, and it wasn't just her feelings on the line, not when there was their jobs and Wes to think about. "Is this just sex for you? Once we're back in the Northern Isles, are we going to pretend this didn't happen? I mean, if it is, tell me, I can accept it. But I need to know now."

"No ... Poppy, no." His hand snaked around her and pulled her to him. His scent and the warmth of his skin enveloped her. "This isn't just sex. I swear." She could feel his heart beating like a drum against her cheek. "I will prove it to you."

"What? No, Rorik you don't have to—"

"Please. Let me think a moment." He paused, taking in a breath. "Tomorrow, I will come to your room earlier."

"You will? But what about the king and queen? Isn't there some big event with the mayor tomorrow night? You need to be with them for the entire evening."

"The queen has decided to cut their attendance short because she's been feeling more fatigued. She and the king will come back right after the dinner, and we will depart the next day as scheduled."

"Oh." She did notice Queen Sybil seemed more listless as

the tour progressed. "Okay then. Should I order dinner or something?"

He shook his head. "No. We shall be heading out."

"O-out?"

"Yes. On a *real* date." His chest rumbled. "But make sure to dress ... warmly."

Warmly? Why? She was about to ask him when he held her tighter and lifted her up into his arms.

"Trust me." He walked them over to the bed. "And I promise that by this time tomorrow, everything will make sense."

Poppy checked the mirror for what seemed like the hundredth time, then plopped back down on the bed. Still, the thrum of excitement coursed through her veins, and she could hardly stop from fidgeting. She'd been waiting the entire day for tonight, and soon, Rorik would be standing outside her door. Then he would knock and—

The knocking sound jolted her, and she nearly fell off the bed.

"Oof!" Thankfully, she managed to steady herself on her feet. She scrambled for the door and threw it open.

"Good evening, Poppy," Rorik greeted.

Oh my. Her stomach flipped in excitement seeing him filling up the doorway. He looked incredibly handsome, too, wearing a white button-down shirt, a green sweater, and dark trousers. "G-good evening," she stammered.

"You look lovely this evening." His appreciative gaze swept over her from head to toe.

"Thanks." As he requested, she'd dressed warmly in a long-sleeved jumper dress, thick leggings, extra socks, and boots. "I, uh, should I get my coat and purse?"

"Yes, please." He stepped inside.

She turned and grabbed her things from the bed. "Is everything okay? Are you sure you can leave the hotel even though the king and queen will be back early?"

"I am sure. Niklas has been briefed about the situation and promises to be on alert the entire night and call me should anything happen."

"Oh, okay." Her nerves settled somewhat as she put her coat on. "Okay, I'm ready. Shall we head out?"

"Yes."

He offered her his arm which she took, but she frowned when he began to lead her out toward her balcony. "Rorik? The door's that way."

"I know." A smile spread across his lips as they stepped out. "I thought we could explore Venice. From above."

"A-a-bove?" She gasped. "Do you mean like ... flying?"

"Yes. I shall carry you in my arms and Cloak us as we fly over the city."

That sounded amazing. And terrifying. "Er, are you sure ..."

"Yes," he said confidently. "My dragon wishes to spend time with you as well."

"Y-your dragon?" Although Wesley often referred to his cheetah in the third person, she wasn't really sure what that meant, but she didn't think it was an entirely different being. "W-will I be safe? With your dragon, I mean?"

"There is no other creature you would be safer with." A

deep, audible rumbled sounded from his chest. "Do you trust me?"

"Yes." It came out so easily, she surprised herself. "I trust you."

He moved behind her and slipped his arms around her torso. Leaning down, he whispered. "You do not know how happy that makes me feel."

The words made her shiver. "I'm scared, though."

"Do not be. We will not let you go."

This time, she shivered, but for a different reason.

"Close your eyes."

She did as he said and he began to walk them forward. There was a tingle in the air as something warm settled over her, covering her. Her feet lifted off the ground and then her body launched upwards. She screamed, her stomach dipped, and finally she opened her eyes.

"Oh ... my Lord!" She was flying! But more than that, two gigantic arms wrapped around her, securing her to a massive scaly body.

The dragon soared high up in the air, then began a gentle descent to the city. Lights outlined the buildings and the Grand Canal that split the island in two. The sight of the city from this high up took her breath away.

They flew to the tip of the city, then made a U-turn, following the outer edge of the island. Once they completed the full circle, they made a beeline for the Grand Canal. The dragon stayed as low as it could without knocking into the buildings. Poppy watched in wonder as they passed over the Rialto Bridge, and the tourists and the gondoliers barely looked up, unaware of what was above them. When they finished going through the main canal, the dragon slowed, then veered off toward the largest open space in Venice—St. Mark's Square. As they came closer, the pigeons, probably sensing the presence of a larger creature coming near them, scattered and flew away. She squeezed her eyes shut, and before she knew it, her feet landed on solid ground.

"Did you enjoy that?"

She leaned back into Rorik's solid, human chest. "Yes, very much." Enjoy might have been too mild a world. It was exhilarating. "Are we still Cloaked?"

"Yes."

She turned in his arms, placing her hands on his chest. "I wasn't sure the first time I saw you, but I guess I wasn't seeing things." She gripped the lapels of his shirt. "Your clothes shift with you." Robbie's and Wesley's didn't do that.

"Yes, another advantage of being a fabled shifter." He loosened his grip around her but didn't let go and instead moved his hand down to hers.

"Come," he said, threading their fingers together. They walked over to a secluded alley off the side of the square. Rorik glanced around, seemingly to make sure no one could see them, then let go of her hand. "There," he said.

"Rorik ... that was the most amazing thing I've ever experienced in my life. Thank you."

His face lit up. "I'm glad you enjoyed it." He tucked her hand into his arm, and they began to walk out of the alley. "Once we are back in the Northern Isles, I can give you a tour around the country. It's not very big, and we could do it in a day. Wesley can join us, if he wishes, and I'll take you to my ancestral home in the south. My father will want to meet you."

Her mind buzzed as she digested his words. He wanted

her to meet his father! And to bring Wesley, too. Surely that meant he was serious about her and wasn't just stringing her along. "I would like that."

"Excellent. Now, I have made reservations at a restaurant nearby. Hopefully you have an appetite?"

"I do," she said.

"Come then." They strode out hand in hand and walked over to one of the many open air eateries along the edge of the square. A jovial host greeted them and led them to a table in front where they had a view of St. Mark's Basilica.

Dinner was marvelous, not that Poppy paid much mind to the food. No, her attention was completely on Rorik. He seemed almost a different person out here. More carefree. Less rigid. And she did enjoy his stories about his childhood and adventures with King Aleksei and the Dragon Guard.

"... and as we saw the poor kitten struggling to stay afloat in a river, a loud splash surprised us all."

"Splash?" She put her wine glass down. "What was it? Did something swoop in and take the kitten?"

"In a way." The grin on his face made him look years younger. "It was Stein. He jumped into the freezing water and rescued the poor creature."

"*Stein?*" Good thing she wasn't drinking her wine or she would have choked on it. "He went in before all of you?"

He laughed. "Yes. Without any hesitation or delay."

"Huh." Maybe the queen was right. Somewhere inside his stony exterior was a soft underbelly.

"Poppy," he began as he took her hands in his. "There is something I must tell you."

"What?" The seriousness in his tone pricked her curiosity.

"Something important. Poppy, I have wanted you since the moment I laid eyes on you."

"You have?"

"Yes, and that's because—" A ringing sound cut him off. "Oh, for Thor's sake! I ask for one evening—"

"No, go ahead and pick it up, it might be Niklas."

Rorik fished his phone from his pocket. "This is Ror— What's wrong?" His ruddy eyebrows drew together. "*Mother Frigga*! I am on my way." His face twisted in fury.

"Rorik?" She could practically feel the rage coming off him. "Is something the mat—"

"No time!" He grabbed her hand and pulled her up from the chair, then began to drag her out into the square.

"Rorik?" His arms wrapped around her in a vise-like grip. "Rorik, what's—" She screamed as her feet left the ground, and once again they shot into the air like a rocket.

What was going on?

CHAPTER 13

As his dragon raced back to the hotel with Poppy in its arms, Rorik could barely contain the rage coursing through his veins. The emotion had come so swiftly and now threatened to overcome him. And to think he was about to confess his feelings to his mate right when the call came.

Some intruders had broken into the suite, Melina Gunnarson had said through the phone's receiver. *The king is safe, and so is the queen and prince, but Niklas was wounded badly.*

They would pay, whoever it was that threatened his king and hurt his brother-in-arms.

It was a good thing Venice was small as, within moments, they approached the balcony leading to the king's suite. He shifted back, tucking his dragon deep inside him, and landed on the tiled floor in full human form. Gently, he placed Poppy on her feet, then rushed toward the open double-doors that led into the main suite.

Shock sent his system into overdrive as he saw the state of the room. It lay in shambles, broken glass and furniture strewn about, and the carpet soaked with water. The wall on the far side had its wallpaper scorched off and the smell of burnt ash hung in the air.

"What happened?" he roared. "Tell me—Niklas!" He rushed to the other dragon who lay prone on the couch. The queen sat next to him, holding a towel seeped in red. "H-how is he?"

"I don't know," Queen Sybil choked out, her face white as a sheet. "We took the weapon out." She nodded as the bloody knife on the floor. "But he's not healing. I can't—I can't reach him through our mental link."

Niklas, he screamed, but he didn't answer. Kneeling next to him, he touched his forehead. "He's got a fever."

"The knife must have been poisoned," King Aleksei, who stood behind the couch, deduced.

"But with what? Bloodsbane?" It was the only substance known to harm shifters.

"No, something—Poppy?" King Aleksei's head swung toward the balcony. "What are you doing out there?"

"She was with me," Rorik said. *Please,* he said to the king and queen. *I can explain, but not now.*

"Y-Your Majesties." Poppy rushed in and then gasped when she saw Niklas. "No ... oh no. Your Majesty, the prince—"

"Is safe, with Ingrid downstairs in the manager's office." The queen shot Rorik a quizzical look. "Poppy, could you go and check with Melina regarding the doctor? The manager called him, but that was a while ago."

"Of course, Your Majesty." She quickly dashed out the door.

"What happened?" Rorik asked. "Tell me."

The king ran a hand through his hair. "We were just getting back from the dinner. Niklas walked into the suite, and they were there. Waiting for us." His jaw hardened. "Three men. It happened so fast. There was a struggle. I don't know ..."

"I ran for Alric's room and grabbed him and Ingrid and flew them away," Queen Sybil continued. "Once I secured them with our security team downstairs, I came back up here. Niklas was on the floor, that knife in his shoulder. Aleksei ... he was floating in the air."

"I could not move." The king rubbed his jaw. "It was like being held together with vices. Nor could I call on my dragon."

"They were using a wand." Queen Sybil's voice shook.

"The Wand?" His hands curled into fists. "But we have it secured back in the Northern Isles!" Only the king, Thoralf, and he knew its exact location.

"No, not The Wand. Another wand," the queen qualified. "It looked different I think. I don't know, it was so fast. I saw Aleksei and that they were about to stab him, too, and I let out a burst of fire, first at the one holding the wand, then the other two. The sprinklers came on and it turned to chaos. I think ... I think they all ran out onto the balcony and jumped into the canal."

"I found two dead bodies outside, both badly burned," King Aleksei spat.

"And the third?"

"Gone. Along with the wretched magical weapon."

Rorik kicked an overturned chair in rage. "Bastards!"

"Rorik, calm down," the queen urged. "Getting angry isn't going to help."

"I will find these fiends," he vowed. "I don't care what it takes. I should go and search the city for any trace of the last assassin."

"He's probably long gone by now," King Aleksei said.

"I should have been here. To protect you and—"

"The doctor is here!" Poppy announced as she burst through the door. An older man with wiry white hair followed in behind her, black bag in one hand.

"Over here," Queen Sybil called.

"Please, doctor," Rorik began. "Do what you can to—"

"Rorik, let's head outside," the king said. "Now."

"Yes, my king." He glanced over at Niklas as the queen stepped aside to let the doctor work. He could feel Poppy's eyes on him, but ignored her and followed King Aleksei out into the hallway. "Your Majesty," he began. "If you wish for me to resign—"

"Resign? Good gods, why would I do that? The Dragon Guard is shorthanded enough as it is." The king glanced down at his outfit. "So, you and Poppy ..."

"Yes, I was out with her. And I'm sorry, that was my mistake. I should not have left the hotel at all. This is all my fault."

"Rorik, that's not what I—"

"Aleksei, Rorik." Queen Sybil wiped her hands down her dress as she strode out of the room, Poppy behind her.

The sight of the blood staining the queen's ballgown

reminded Rorik of Niklas's perilous situation. "How is he? What did the doctor say?"

"I can't understand him, I'm afraid, but he looked pretty shocked. But he's working on him right now, probably stitching him up to stop the bleeding."

"His human side should respond to normal medical procedures," the king said. "But the wand ..."

"Could it be we have a copycat wand?" Queen Sybil asked.

"No, otherwise I would not have my dragon anymore," King Aleksei deduced. "But I could not move, and my dragon would not respond. It's as if the magic in it trapped my animal, but I didn't feel it drain away, like what happened to my father."

Rorik felt some relief at that. If King Aleksei lost his dragon, too, then the kingdom would be thrown into chaos as Prince Alric was too young to rule.

Queen Sybil's silvery eyes narrowed. "If Aristaeum had the power to create one wand, then it's possible there are others."

"The thought of such a thing is terrifying." King Aleksei's mouth pulled back into a grim line. "Sybil, you should contact Christina back in Blackstone. She and the rest of your family should be informed of the events of tonight."

"Right. I'll do that now." The queen strode back into the suite, but not before giving Poppy a sympathetic glance.

"My king ... I am sorry—"

"We can talk about that later." He placed a hand on his shoulder. "Niklas will pull through. He is strong."

"I should call Gideon. He needs to know."

"I shall be the one to do that."

"I am his superior and therefore—"

"And I am his king." King Aleksei didn't look like he was in the mood to argue. "Attend to your duties here. Secure the hotel, question witnesses, and find out who tried to kill me and my family." His tone was deadly serious.

Rorik bowed. "I will, my king."

King Aleksei nodded at him, then paused. *And when this is all over, you can apologize for not telling me you found your mate. Perhaps I will forgive you for that, my friend.* He lifted an eyebrow at him, then turned and headed into the suite.

Poppy curtseyed as he walked by. Once the king disappeared into the room, she flew to his side, her arms winding around him. "Oh, Rorik, are you all right?"

He didn't know how to answer that. The king could have died tonight. And Niklas ... it was all his fault. "I should have been here."

"What?"

"If I had been here, I might have stopped them."

"Or you could be the one bleeding out on that couch." Releasing her grip, she turned him to face her. Her dark eyes pleaded up at him. "Rorik, listen to me. None of this is your fault."

"Isn't it? I am the captain of the Dragon Guard. Though I did not ask for this duty, I carry it out nonetheless. And I failed. Failed my king and country." *Failed my brothers.*

"You can't be responsible for everything all the time."

"But I am." He swallowed hard and closed his eyes. He knew he should not have gone out. They should have stayed here. He did not blame her, of course. The burden was on him. He wanted desperately to tell her how he felt and who she was to him.

And he didn't even get to do that. Was there a place for a mate in his life? What if she had been in that room and he had to choose between protecting her and the king? The very thought turned his blood cold. *Perhaps it was better for her to be with another.*

His dragon railed at him and scratched its claws on his inside. *Mine!*

Poppy could do better. She should be with someone who wouldn't put her life in danger or have to choose to save another in her stead. *Like Lars of House Aumont.* Or any other man who would love her enough to pick her over anyone else.

The dragon roared furiously. *Mine!*

"Rorik?" Poppy said in a quiet voice. "Talk to me."

"I ... I should attend to my duties." He gently pried her hands off him.

"Rorik, please! Don't do this."

"I am not doing anything." Not anymore. Not with her.

"You're pulling away from me ... I can feel it. Why?"

"The trail might go cold. I must go and catch the assassin." Walking away was the hardest thing he'd ever done, but he managed it. One foot at a time, one in front of the other.

He ignored his dragon's cries of pain. *She will not be safe with us.*

Their enemies were still out there. *We've become negligent in the last two years.* Did they really think the Knights of Aristaeum would just forget about them? It seemed they were only biding their time, waiting for the opportunity to strike.

But he would not let them. The moment he became a Dragon Guard, he made a vow to protect his king. He also promised Thoralf when he left that he would fulfill his duties as captain. *I promise, I'll catch those bastards.* From now on, his duty would always come first.

And that meant there was no space for a mate in his life.

CHAPTER 14

Poppy stood in the hallway for what seemed like forever. She blinked, not knowing what to do. Rorik didn't say anything, but then, he didn't have to. She could feel it in her heart—he was walking away from her. From what they had shared. For good.

Maybe she was wrong. *He just needs some time.* The events of tonight must have shaken him to his very core. She didn't know how, but she sensed his rage and anxiety as if they were her own feelings. Just like she could tell he was about to tell her something important and life changing back at the restaurant.

I have wanted you since the moment I laid eyes on you.

The door opening behind her shook her out of her thoughts. It was the doctor, looking haggard and weary. He looked at her and smiled weakly, then said something in Italian.

Though she couldn't understand what it was, she could tell that it wasn't bad news. "*Mi dispiace* ... patient ... okay?"

"*Sì.*" He wiped the sweat from his forehead with his sleeve. "Okay."

"Thank you ... *grazie.*" She walked past him and was about to head back into the suite when she heard the king and queen's voices. *I can't face them right now.* Niklas was fine, he probably needed some rest, so instead, she decided to go to her room and get some sleep. Maybe in the morning, Rorik would seek her out once he had some time to calm down and think.

Though she barely slept, she managed to get up early anyway. As they prepared for their departure, the queen didn't say much to her, except to let her know Niklas was recovering but not in full health yet. She could hardly look Queen Sybil in the eye, as it was obvious to everyone last night that she and Rorik had been out on a date. She just did her job, took care of the prince, and packed up everything so they could head to the airport.

To her surprise, when she got on board with the prince's things, Niklas was already there in one of the seats in the back, and so was Gideon.

"Niklas! How are you feeling?" She rushed over to them. "And Gideon, what are you doing here?"

"I flew over as soon as Rorik called." There was a tightness in his expression, especially when he glanced over at his twin. "With Niklas down, he needed another Dragon Guard here."

Niklas snorted. "I told you, it's just a scratch. I'm fine. I'm sure I can still do my duty." He winced when he tried to get up.

"Stay down, moron," Gideon barked. "Your body seems to have expelled most of whatever poison they used on you, but not all of it. It might take another few hours before you're fully healed."

"I'm glad you're okay, Niklas." *And I'm sorry.*

"I'm a tough guy." He grinned at her. "Say, where's Rorik? And how was your date last night—ow!" Gideon elbowed him and shot him a dirty look.

"Um, I need to get ready for Prince Alric," she muttered and trudged back to the front of the plane. She tried not to think about Rorik as she set up the prince's seat, but each time someone came into the cabin, her heart did a little leap hoping it was him, but ended up disappointed as it turned out to be someone else.

Once the king, queen, and Prince Alric were settled in, she, too, sat down, and when the door closed, she knew that Rorik would not be joining them. She slumped back in her seat and swallowed the lump in her throat. *He's probably got a lot of work to do with the local authorities,* she thought. This was a diplomatic matter, after all. Or he was chasing down the remaining assassin? *I hope he catches that bastard!*

The flight back home was silent, and there was obviously a dark cloud over all of them. As soon as they landed and she deplaned behind the royal family, the one bright spot in her otherwise dreary morning arrived.

"Mum!" Wesley bounded out of the SUV parked on the tarmac and ran toward her.

"Wes!" She caught him and held him tight. "Oh, Wes." Tears pricked at her eyes. "I missed you so much."

"Me too," he whispered.

Poppy didn't want to let go yet, but did so anyway when he loosened his grip. "How are you? How was school? And the dorms? Did you get enough to eat?"

"Mum, I'm fine! They—" He glanced behind her. "Niklas!"

Turning her head, she saw Niklas descending the stairs. Gideon guided him down, but when he saw Wesley, he waved his brother away and made his way to them unassisted.

"Hey, little man, what's shaking?"

Wesley swallowed audibly. "Gideon said he had to leave right away last night because you were hurt. Are you all right?"

"You mean this?" He nodded at the bandage around his shoulder. "*Pffft*! That's nothing. Just a flesh wound."

"Are we ready to leave?" Queen Sybil asked. "I'm so looking forward to being home."

"Just a moment, My Queen." Gideon nodded to the landing strip, where the second jet was now taxiing toward them. Minutes later, it stopped behind their plane. The door opened and the rest of the delegation arrived, including Rorik.

Poppy couldn't stop herself from tracking him as he strode toward them. Her throat went dry, and she took a deep breath as he passed her. He continued walking, making his way to the SUV in front of the line of vehicles that would escort the royal family and their entourage back to Odelia. He opened the door and stood by it, keeping his gaze locked ahead.

"I should get going," Poppy said. "I'll see you back at home, Wes." She jogged back toward the queen and took Prince Alric from her. As they passed by Rorik, he didn't move or even acknowledge her, like he used to do. There was no knowing glance, no secret smile.

Her stomach tied itself in knots at his snub, but she pushed it away for now. *He was just trying to act professional in front of everyone.* She couldn't even imagine the pressure on him now, especially when the king had nearly been assassinated on his watch. Her heart went out to him, and she vowed that once they had a chance to sit down and iron this out, she would do her best to support him and let him know this wasn't his fault.

Poppy practiced the words she would say to Rorik when she saw him. But two weeks passed, and there was no trace of the captain of the Dragon Guard. At least, she saw no sign of him.

But even before the tour, she and Rorik never crossed paths in their daily routine, so maybe he would come to her when she was done for the day. She even waited in the living room of their apartment each night after Wesley had gone to bed, just in case he decided to come by. But there was no knock on the door. When the first Saturday of the month came, she went with the queen and Prince Alric to the Children's Foundation, but it was only Gideon and Stein who had accompanied them.

And now she felt utterly pathetic because even after all this time, her heart still held hope that she would see him.

"Mum, can we go see Niklas?" Wesley asked one evening as she came home.

"Niklas?" She put her things down on the consul table, then plopped down on the couch. Her feet ached as Prince Alric had been especially rambunctious today. "Whatever for?" That seemed strange, as he'd never shown an interest in Gideon's twin before. During the time she'd been away, Wesley did manage to make a few friends at school and spent less time at the library, but he still went there to finish his homework some days. Poppy had dropped by a few times, hoping to run into Rorik.

"I want to see if he's okay now, after his injury."

"Oh, right." Though she had asked Gideon about his brother, the dragon shifter only told them that he was fine and fully recovered. "I suppose we should have checked up on him." The memory of Niklas's pale face and all that blood made her stomach turn.

"Yes! Let's go!" He tugged at her hand and pulled her up.

"Now? And where are we going exactly?" she asked, puzzled. "And shouldn't we tell Niklas to expect us?"

"He knows we're coming." He practically pushed her out the door. "C'mon, let's hurry."

"Wesley, we should—wait!" But her son had already dashed down the hallway. *Oh, my aching feet.* But it wasn't like she could let him roam around the palace. Surely there were places here where people couldn't just wander into, and she didn't want him to get lost. On their first day, Melina had only given them a tour of the main hall and the residential areas, since there was no need for them to see the entire place.

"Wesley!" she called, spying him scamper down a hall she'd never entered. "Wait!" She followed him deeper into the palace, toward the north side if her orientation was correct. As she continued on, she noticed that this section seemed to be older. The bare stone walls held no precious art pieces, nor did the floors have plush carpeting.

"Mum!" Wesley waved at her. "Come on!"

She blew out a breath and went after him, picking up her pace. As she turned the next corner, she bumped right into a stone wall. Before she could fall back, a pair of hands gripped her shoulders to steady her.

"I—oh." It wasn't a wall. It was Rorik, staring down at her, bright green eyes flashing with surprise before breaking their gaze. Her stomach tightened. "Rorik, I—"

"Pardon me, Ms. Baxter." His hands released their grip, then he sidestepped her and began to walk away.

Poppy closed her eyes, her throat burning. *Pathetic,* she told herself. *You're so pathetic.*

"Mum?"

She pressed her lips together before she spoke. "Wes. Where's Niklas? And where are we?"

"We're in the North Tower, where the Dragon Guard live." He tugged at her jumper. "Mum?"

Slowly, she lowered her gaze, thankful the tears hadn't come yet. "Yes, Wes?"

"Rorik ... are you friends?"

"No, Wes." She smiled weakly. "We're not friends."

"Why not?"

How was she supposed to answer that? "I—"

"Hey, guys!"

Poppy looked up and saw Gideon descending a set of stairs at the end of the hall. "Gideon. Where's Niklas?"

"He's upstairs, getting some snacks ready. Say," he glanced around, "did you happen to see Rorik? He said he was heading out."

"We did, and he left," Poppy said quickly, then ushered

Wes forward when he started to open his mouth. "C'mon, Wes, Niklas is waiting. We should go."

Wes looked up at her, eyes narrowing. She ignored him. "So, this is where you live, Gideon?"

"Yes," he replied. "Welcome to the North Tower. The Dragon Guard have lived here since Helgeskar Palace was built hundreds of years ago by King Dordund the Third. C'mon, I'll give you a tour."

Though her heart felt like it had cracked into a thousand pieces, Poppy managed a smile. "Sounds great. Lead on."

CHAPTER 15

The sound of metal crashing against metal, the feeling of his lungs and muscles burning, and the smell of sweat should have satisfied Rorik and his dragon. Indeed, there was nothing he enjoyed more than a rigorous training session. But it seemed not even going up against a skilled opponent could make him forget the thoughts that had been plaguing his mind since they arrived back from the tour.

"Argh!" he roared as he brought the sword down on Ranulf. The other dragon shifter raised his axe to block it, the contact between the blades setting off sparks. Rorik pushed with all his might, and although Ranulf dug his heels in to stop from falling back, the slick, slushy snow sent him sliding back.

His dragon snarled, urging him to take advantage of the situation. Rorik advanced with a growl and swung the sword, the tip slashing across Ranulf's chest, the blood blooming across his tattooed skin. The trainee barely even flinched, and instead he pushed himself off the ground, backflipped, and landed on his feet.

Rorik charged, making a motion to swing the sword again when he heard Stein in his head.

Enough. The weapons master's gravelly voice abraded his mind like sandpaper. *Rorik! Stop.*

But Rorik's beast let out a shrieking howl and refused to back down.

"Bring it on, sir," Ranulf goaded. "I can take it."

Stein stepped forward. "I think we are done for the day."

"But—"

"Dismissed," he barked at Ranulf. "All of you," he added to the rest of the trainees.

Ranulf huffed, but trudged over to where he dropped his axe and picked it up. However, instead of following the others, he came over to Rorik. "It was an honor, sir, to spar with you." He wiped the blood from the healing cut on his chest with his palm. "You are as great a warrior as they say you are."

Rorik stared at him, not sure what to say at first. "You are a good fighter, but you did not consider the weather conditions." The late winter snowstorm had started hours ago, but learning to fight in adverse environments was part of the Dragon Guard training so they continued with the training. It had slowed down now, but the snow piled up around them and as they trained, turned to a slushy, slippery mess.

"I will remember that." Ranulf bowed to him and then to Stein before slogging off to join his comrades.

Once they were all gone, Rorik spoke. "Why suddenly stop the training? We were just getting started."

Stein snorted. *It looked more like you were about to end it.*

Where is your control? I've seen you train and fight for real. And I do not know what that *was.*

He gritted his teeth. "If they are to become one of us, then we cannot take it easy on them. The royal family must be protected at all times. There is no failure for a Dragon Guard." But then again, he almost did fail. He vowed to find the fiends who tried to assassinate the king. It was the only thing fueling him these days, keeping him going despite the shame in his mind and the gaping hole in his heart.

Stein's eyes turned hard as granite. *I know that, but could you please not kill my trainees? I have spent months turning them from bumbling idiots to competent morons, and I do not have the patience to start from scratch.*

"I was not trying to kill them."

Tell that to your dragon. "Come, we shall be late for our meeting with his Majesty."

Rorik was glad that Stein didn't say anything else as they slogged through the slush. He'd avoided the palace as much as he could in the last couple of days, even canceling his usual meetings with staff in his office and using the balcony from his apartments to go in and out, just so he didn't risk running into Poppy like he did the other day when she came to the tower. Shock was a mild word to describe how he felt, and it took every bit of his willpower to walk away from her.

His dragon scratched him with its claws at the thought of her. Its mood had turned even fouler as of late, but he pushed it deep inside or just ignored it. Today, however, the aggression had built up so much that he needed an outlet which was how he ended up joining Stein's training session.

They headed into the palace and then made their way to

the king's office. As they drew nearer, they saw King Aleksei walking toward them.

"Ah, Stein, Rorik, good, I was just about to call for you," he greeted as the two men bowed to him. "Gideon informed me that he found some crucial new information that cannot wait. I am on the way to the library now, I thought we might meet there instead. He's already called Niklas. Let us make haste."

The library was the last place Rorik wanted to be, but he had no choice but to follow his king. When they arrived, though, there was no sign of the twins.

The king glanced around. "Where—"

A loud thud interrupted him, followed by several more thumps and crashes and a yelp. Rorik's instincts immediately propelled him toward the source of the sound, which his shifter hearing deduced came from the shelves on the right side of the room. The first row was empty, but when he turned into the second, he spied the pile of books on the floor —and a small figure dangling from the highest shelf.

Wesley.

His fingers began to slip, and Rorik leapt forward and snatched him before he fell to the ground. The boy would heal if he broke a limb, but he would still be in pain, something he would not be able to bear.

"What were you doing up there, Wesley?" he scolded.

The boy squirmed in his arms. "Let me go!"

"Had I not been here, you could have been hurt."

"I don't need help from you!" Wesley hissed, then scraped his claws down his arm, causing Rorik to let go of him. He landed on his feet.

"Wesley!" The scratch was minimal and did not break

the skin, but it caught him off guard. "What in Odin's beard did you do that for?"

"I told you, I don't need help, especially not from you." His voice trembled, but he stood firm. And for once, Rorik did not feel fear or anxiety from him; no, he radiated pure fury.

"Where is your mother?"

"Don't you dare mention her," he growled.

"Listen—"

"I hate you. I never want to see you ever. When you came to the park, I thought you were different."

"Different?" What did he mean?

"Different from my dad. But now I see you're just like him."

His spine stiffened, and a pain stabbed in his chest. "Wes—"

"You made her cry." His voice turned soft and low. "She thinks I can't hear it because she's hiding in her bathroom, but I can. Every. Night."

Oh, Wesley. Poppy. He had made a mess of things. *I shouldn't have gotten involved with her in the first place.*

"Rorik?" It was the king. "What is going on?"

Mother Frigga. "Your Majesty, I can—" But before he could continue, Wesley dashed away, running past King Aleksei and Stein.

"Rorik—"

"Is Gideon here?" he interrupted. "We should start the meeting." He strode off into the main hall where, thankfully, Gideon and Niklas were both already standing by one of the large tables looking at a leather-bound book propped up on a wooden stand.

"Your Majesty," Gideon greeted. "Thank you for coming. I had to go fetch Niklas."

King Aleksei marched over to them, Stein right behind him. "Tell me what is this new information you have uncovered."

"Ah, yes." Gideon flipped the pages on the book. "When Niklas described the events of that night in Venice to me and told me of the second wand, I remembered something that came up in my previous research while searching for a cure for Prince Harald." He turned the book around to face them. "Here." On the spread was a drawing of a long, thin wand with a jeweled head. Rorik could see the similarities in its design with The Wand, though the runes inscribed all over the body looked different; cruder, almost.

"That's the wand," King Aleksei gasped. "The one they used to hold me and my dragon."

"I recognized it too," Niklas said.

"Why are you only telling us this now?" Rorik asked.

"I didn't know what it was at the time, but I did tell Thoralf about it. In fact, he investigated it. When he found nothing, we just assumed it was another dead end and went to the next lead."

King Aleksei's brows furrowed. "What do you know about this second wand?"

Gideon picked up his tablet PC and turned it to them. On the screen was a sepia-toned photograph of the same wand. "This photo is from the archives of the Oxford Department of Anthropology, taken in 1915. The wand was in the possession of a tribe in the Assyrian Mountains, who used it for their rituals. The researcher who found it figured out that the tribe couldn't have made it because they didn't have any metallurgical knowledge, nor did the mountains contain any silver or mineral. That means it had to come from somewhere else. So, I traced it back and discovered that it predates The Wand by at least several hundred years, according to the drawing."

"But you said it was a dead end?"

Gideon nodded. "Thoralf found the tribe, but the elders told him that it had been acquired—i.e., stolen—by the local government a few months ago to be put in their National Museum. But when he went to the museum, they said they didn't have the wand. And that's where the trail goes cold."

"The Knights must have stolen it," Stein deduced.

"But you said it predates The Wand by a few hundred years," the king asked.

"Yes, which is why we didn't pursue it any further. But," Gideon put his tablet PC down and let out a breath, "what if this wand was an early design or the basis of The Wand? What if it took The Knights hundreds of years and many tries, but eventually, they did create a wand that could separate a shifter from his animal?"

"It's a good theory. This early prototype could have been a precursor, as it only trapped my dragon so I could not access it, but not completely destroyed it." King Aleksei's eyes darkened. "But now I fear what else they have uncovered and what other type of anti-shifter magic is loose out there."

"That's a chilling thought," Niklas said. "And The Knights are smart and patient. They don't strike unless they know they can do maximum damage."

"We must be vigilant," the king declared. "Any news on the assassin?"

Rorik winced inwardly. "I'm afraid not, Your Majesty.

I've been in contact with the Venice police and the mayor's office, as well as a representative of the Italian Government. They have CCTV footage, but the only thing they could deduce is that the three men must have come in by a private speedboat from the mainland, and the remaining attacker blended in with the tourist crowd to make his way out undetected." He still seethed, thinking of that night. If he had been there, then he could have easily pursued the fiend.

"There is one thing that has been on my mind these very last weeks." The king then switched to their mental link. *You four are my most trusted advisers, so this information does not leave this circle.*

Of course, everyone replied.

No one outside the delegation knew that Sybil and I were going to make our excuses to leave early that evening, not even the mayor himself, as we did not want to embarrass him or cause an international incident. As the queen and I planned, right after eating, she pretended to faint and get sick.

Wait, Gideon interjected. *Do you mean to say the assassins were already waiting there and attacked at the right time?*

Couldn't they have already slipped in early and lucked out? Stein asked.

Ingrid put Alric to bed at eight, then she says she came out to the living room at around eight thirty to have her evening meal before going back into his room at nine. There was no place for three men to hide in that suite, the king said.

We arrived at the hotel at nine thirty, which means they knew we were coming in early, Niklas deduced. *They were standing right there in the middle of the living room, and definitely weren't surprised.*

They were tipped off, Rorik said, gnashing his teeth. *We were betrayed by our own.* Odin's beard. Now they had to deal with someone inside the palace betraying them to their enemies.

That's what I am afraid of, the king said. *But that is why I have asked for outside help.*

Outside help? Rorik echoed.

Yes. As you know, the queen's sister-in-law, Christina Lennox, runs the Blackstone arm of the Shifter Protection Agency. She and I spoke a few minutes ago, and she suggested that we plant one of her undercover agents to try to find the traitor among us.

Indignation burst inside Rorik. But he had no one to blame but himself. The king had obviously lost his trust in him, which is why he was bringing in someone from the outside. Still, he had to make his objection known. *Is that wise, My King? An outsider infiltrating the palace to find a mole? Surely, we can ferret out this traitor ourselves.*

This traitor has concealed himself well within our ranks, the king replied. *Not to mention, we ourselves might be biased. An objective outsider is what we need to find this snake in the grass. In any case, it is already done, and the agent will arrive here as quickly as it can be arranged. My decision on this is final.*

Of course, Your Majesty, Rorik conceded.

"Now," the king began in his normal tone. "Gideon, let me know when you find out anything more about the wand or any other wands. You're dismissed." He looked at Rorik. "But I would like a private word, for a moment."

Everyone else bowed and filed out of the library. The king asking for a private word from his captain wasn't unusual, but Rorik had a gut feeling this would be no ordinary conversation. "Yes, Your Majesty?"

Rorik, he began. *Poppy was part of the delegation. She knew our schedule, and she's very close to the queen making her privy to certain information.*

His dragon roared in protest. "No!" He slammed his fists down, then realized he had spoken out loud. Slinking back, he said, *She is not the traitor!*

King Aleksei's expression did not change. *How can you be sure?*

She did not know that you were planning to come back early. I told her myself because it gave us the opportunity to go out on our date.

"Ah yes, the date." The king was smirking now. "You still owe me that apology for not telling me who she was to you."

Rorik puffed his cheeks and let out a breath, then sank down on one of the chairs. "My King ... Aleksei, I am sorry for that. And sorry for everything." He buried his face in his hands.

"Rorik, I have watched you these past weeks. Felt your dragon's anger and the conflict inside you. And then I saw Poppy looking all glum, I just knew it."

"Knew what?"

"That you were being a damned idiot!" The king slapped him on the head. "What the hell are you thinking, staying away from your mate like that? You are hurting her and hurting yourself!"

He looked up and rubbed the back of his head. "This was all my fault. You were nearly killed! And Niklas, he could have died too!"

"But I survived, and so did he. This is not your fault. It was The Knights who chose to attack us."

"But you could have."

"But we didn't."

"If I had been there—"

"Cease!" The king cut him off. "We can continue back and forth like this, arguing in circles, but it does not change the fact that Poppy is your mate."

"I don't know what to do." He scrubbed his hand down his face. "I have the most important duty in the land. You and Thoralf entrusted me to keep you and your greatest treasures —your family—safe, and I have failed."

"No, you have not failed, not yet. You will prevail, Rorik. You and the rest of the Dragon Guard will find this assassin, The Wand, and The Knights and stop them before they do any more harm to our kind. I know it."

"I promise you, My King. I will."

"So, what is stopping you from claiming your mate?"

He swallowed audibly. "I thought ... if Poppy had been there in that room, I would have saved her first. And I wouldn't have hesitated. Forgive me, My King, for thinking that. But it's true, and that's why I cannot pursue her."

King Aleksei sat on the chair beside him and placed a hand on his shoulder. "Rorik, I know it's quite unfair to you, the way you came to this position. Thoralf leaving put a burden on everyone, but you especially. But you never complained, and you've exceeded all expectations despite all the challenges. And you are a great warrior. Your father trained you well, and I know because I've felt the broad side of Neils's sword many times." He let out a chuckle. "But see, you also need balance. You cannot just go through life with the mindset of a warrior. Yes, you remain strong and hard, but also grow brittle." He gave him a squeeze. "When we fought during the first attack, I thought I was doing Sybil a favor by staying away from her and telling her I didn't need her. But it turns out, I really did need her."

"We all did," Rorik reminded him. "Were it not for her and her dragon, we would have lost."

"True. But that's not the only reason I need her. Having a mate and a family makes me a better person. A better king even, because at the end of the day, what is the point of it all if we cannot fight for those we love and make the world a safer place for them?"

The king's words sunk into him, slowly at first, but then spread through him like wildfire. *Poppy*. He'd been staying away all this time because of his duty and his guilt, but he'd hurt her so badly. Made her cry. His dragon lashed its tail at him. "I need to see her. But what do I do? What do I say?"

King Aleksei laughed. "Well, I hope you're prepared to —Poppy!"

"Prepared to Poppy?" When he saw the king's eyes focus behind him, he turned around.

There she was, standing in the library doorway. "I—Your Majesty!" She curtseyed. "I didn't realize you'd be here."

Rorik immediately saw the strain on her face. "Poppy, what's wrong?"

Her hands wrung together. "H-have you seen Wesley? He didn't come home, and I thought he'd be here with Gideon."

"He hasn't come home yet?" It had been at least half an hour since Wesley ran out.

Her eyes lit up. "He was here then?"

"Yes, but he left." *I hate you* the boy had said. The words stung him straight in the heart, but he would find a way to make it up to him. *I promise, Wesley, I'll never make your mother cry again.*

"M-maybe he just went to the kitchens ... or went to look for Gideon or something." Her lower lip trembled. "I'm sorry to have disturbed you, goodnight."

He stared after her, watching as she disappeared out the doorway. Despite how distraught she'd been, she's never looked lovelier. His heart ached, wanting to be with her so much.

"Good gods, man!" The king exclaimed. "Go after her!"

"What—oh, right! Thank you, Your Majesty." With a quick bow, he ran out the door. "Poppy! Poppy, wait!" He saw her at the end of the hallway, standing by the window. "Poppy, please, can we—what's wrong?"

She clutched something in her hands—clothes, it looked like. When the wind blew her hair away from her face and she shivered, he realized the window was open. "Poppy?"

"Wes was wearing this today." She frowned as she stared down at her hands, then out the window. "Oh no! Wes." Leaning her head out, she called again. "Wes!"

"Mother Frigga!" he cursed. The boy must have shifted and then crawled out. "Poppy, Wes, he—he saw me in the library, and we had a little altercation."

"Altercation?" She fisted the clothes in her hands as she spun to face him. "What do you mean, altercation?"

"He was angry with me. Because I made you cry."

Her face paled. "He heard me."

He swallowed the lump growing in his throat. "And then he ran away ... he must have been distraught."

"Oh no, Wes!" she choked out a cry. "I have to find him. He's out there, and it's snowing. He'll be scared and alone—"

"I'll find him," he vowed. "Do not worry. I will fly over the entire country if I have to." And his dragon agreed. The youngling was under their protection from now on. "Wait in your apartments. I will send word when I find—"

"What? Are you crazy? I'm not letting you go out there and search for him while I sit around twiddling my thumbs."

"You are human," he pointed out, then glanced down at her thin sweater and pants. "You wouldn't last an hour out there in the cold."

"Then I'll put on a coat," she countered. "I'm his mother. Rorik." Those dark eyes pleaded with him. "Take me with you. If you do find him, he might not want to come back with you anyway."

He chewed on his inner cheek. "All right. Get your coat, and meet me in the courtyard."

She was already dashing down the hallway. "Thank you!"

He blew out a breath. Gods, the things he did for the love of his mate.

Flying in dragon form with Poppy in his arms brought back memories from the night in Venice—the happy times anyway, before the assassination attempt. But Rorik vowed that he would do everything in his power to make it up to her and fuse the bond that would link them forever.

Of course, there was a possibility she would reject him because of the way he'd treated her these past weeks. But even if she did, at the very least, he would ensure she was happy and would never have any reason to cry again.

He couldn't fly too fast as he didn't want the wind to freeze Poppy's face off, but then there was no need as the small cub couldn't have gotten too far away, probably not even out of the palace grounds. While Poppy had gone to retrieve her coat, he alerted the rest of the Dragon Guard, and they joined the search with Stein even instructing the trainees to go out on foot. Rorik had taken the northern part of the grounds, as the window Wesley had crawled out of faced north, and that was the likely direction he would have run off to.

"Rorik!" Poppy screamed. "There!"

His dragon swooped lower, its keen eyes searching across the vast field of snow-covered ground. Sure enough, lying on top of a snowbank was a tiny brown and black ball of fur. Gently, he hovered and let her down, before shifting back to his human form.

"Oh, Wes!" She bundled the cheetah cub into her coat. "My poor boy."

"Is he all right?"

"Yes, just passed out. Goodness, he got farther than I thought." She glanced around awkwardly. "Um, thank you for finding him. And bringing me along."

There was so much he wanted to say at this moment. All the words jumbled up in his mind, and his lungs squeezing the air out of his chest made it hard to say them. But then he saw her shivering again. "Come," he said. "Let's get you back."

Before she could protest, he shifted back to his dragon form, then picked her up and flew off. He did not want this night to end without speaking with her and telling her everything in his heart, but would she even give him a chance or slam the door in his face?

His dragon let out a hiss.

And he understood what it was trying to say. *Seize the opportunity*. So, instead of flying back to the main wing of the palace, he made a beeline for the North Tower. He zeroed in on his target—his balcony—then landed with his two human feet on the ground and Poppy in his arms.

"Rorik?" Her entire body was rigid. "Where are we?"

"You are freezing." He shifted his position, so he had an arm slung around her shoulders. "Come inside so you both can get warm. I shall start a fire."

"Fire? What—Rorik?" He didn't allow her to protest and pulled her inside. Her eyes widened. "What is this place?"

"These are my apartments." As captain, he had the top suite and the biggest room in the entire tower. Inside was a massive living area, three bedrooms, a full kitchen, three bathrooms, and one of his favorite features—a real fireplace. As a dragon shifter, he didn't need it, but he loved how cozy it made the room feel.

He led her to the couch, sat her down, and tossed some logs into the fireplace before lighting it. Then he strode to the breakfast nook and picked up the phone, dialing the number to the king and queen's apartments and spoke to Queen Sybil and let her know that Wesley had been found and that the search could be called off. Then, he called the kitchens. "Hello, good evening, this is Rorik. Can I have some hot tea and sandwiches brought to my apartments, please? Thank you." He hung up.

"You don't have to—"

He held up a hand and strode over to her. "How is Wesley?"

Poppy untucked him from her coat. "Tired. And wet."

He grabbed a throw on the couch and held it out. "May I?"

She hesitated, then placed him on the blanket.

"There, there," he cooed, wrapping the soft fabric around him. Walking over to the hearth, he placed Wesley close to the fire. "That should warm you up, *pysen*." Though in old Nordgensprak that meant "runt" or "small one," that had been what his father called him when he was a young boy.

Getting to his feet, he scrounged up his courage and turned to her. Poppy had taken off her coat and had settled onto the couch, rubbing her arms to warm up. Gods, she looked so gorgeous. The firelight played over her skin, making it glow like molten gold. As she lifted her head, those obsidian eyes crashed into him.

"Rorik? Why did you bring us here?"

Slowly, he approached her, as if she was a skittish deer that would leap away at any moment. He sat beside her and settled his hands in his lap. "Poppy, can we talk?"

Her nostrils flared. "I don't know what we have to talk about. I think you've made that pretty clear these last few weeks."

The hurt that flashed in her eyes buckled his confidence, but he wasn't going to give up without a fight. "I know I don't always say the right things. But, please, will you hear me out? Just five minutes of your time."

She took a quick intake of breath. Seconds passed before she nodded.

Thank Thor. "I was raised to be a warrior. To fight and

protect my king, with my own life if I had to. And I failed that night."

"You didn't fail," she said. "And it's not your fault those bastards went after King Aleksei."

"That's what he says. But still, the idea of being a Dragon Guard had been ingrained in me since childhood. My father taught me everything I needed to know to defend myself and my king. Duty came first, always. And I did not grow up knowing how to woo a woman with soft words or grand gestures of love." He heard her heartbeat spike at the mention of the word love, and a spark of hope lit up in him. "That night, in St. Mark's Square, I wanted to tell you something important. I had practiced how so many times in the mirror. And I did not even get to say it to you."

Her mouth parted. "And what is that?"

"You are my mate, Poppy. My fated mate, deemed by the gods to be the other half of my soul."

"M-mate? Like, soulmates?"

"Yes. See, when a shifter meets his intended mate, his animal instinctively knows. It told me, the moment I laid eyes on you."

"You said you wanted me from the very first moment."

"I did." Tentatively, he reached for her hand and breathed a sigh of relief when she did not pull away. "I wanted you. Wanted you to be by my side for the rest of my life. Wanted our souls to bond and be one." Lifting her hand up, he kissed her palm. "And there was one other thing I wanted to say."

"One other thing?" she echoed, her voice barely a whisper.

"I love you, Poppy." She gasped. "I do. I know I have hurt

you and treated you badly. Wesley was right; I'm no different from your ex-husband. I shouldn't have—"

"No, no!" She scooted closer to him, bringing her hands up to cup his face. "You're nothing like Robbie. He tried to exploit Wesley, but you ... you went after him. Kept him safe."

He closed his eyes and nuzzled at her palm. "Forgive me, Poppy. Please. I'll do anything. Say you forgive me."

"I do," she said. "And ... and I love you too."

His heart soared into the stratosphere at her declaration, dragging his dragon with it. His beast whipped its tail in happiness and flapped its wings. "Poppy ..."

She moved into him, sliding her body along his, arms sliding up his chest and to his neck, pulling him down for a kiss. Sweet gods above, it was the most wonderful feeling in the world. Drums pounded in his ears; sparks flashed before his very eyes. Then a tightness wrapped around him, like ribbons binding him, but it did not envelope just him. No, by the time they pulled away, Rorik could feel it. The bond. Poppy.

"What the—" She sucked in a breath and blinked. "What just happened?"

"It's the bond," he said.

"Bond? What bond? Did you know about the bond?"

"Er, kind of? It is supposed to be different for everyone, but I can feel it. Can you?" He placed her hand over his chest. A warmth spread around him as her face lit up.

"I-I do. I can't explain it. But I do."

"So, are you guys mates now?"

Poppy started and jumped away from him. "Wes!"

Wesley, now in human form, stood by the fireplace,

rubbing his eyes as he wrapped the blanket around him. "So? Are you?"

Rorik smiled at Poppy. "Yes, we're truly mates now."

"But you're not in the friend zone, though, are you Rorik?"

"The what?" Poppy exclaimed. "Where on earth did you hear that from?"

"From Niklas," Wes stated. "The night of the party, I overheard him and Gideon talking about Rorik being in the friend zone with you. I thought that was a bad thing because I didn't want you to be friends back then. But then we went to London, and the stuff with Dad happened, and he came to help us, so I said I wouldn't mind if you became friends."

"You did?" Rorik didn't realize Wes had already changed his mind about him then.

"Yeah. But then Mum said you weren't friends anymore. I asked Gideon why Rorik wasn't in the friend zone, and he said that was actually a bad thing, and you needed to be in the *mates* zone. That's when we decided to *Parent Trap* you by inviting Mum to the tower."

"I beg your pardon? Trap us with what?"

Poppy giggled and put a hand on his arm. "I'll tell you later."

"Anyway," Wes continued. "I'm really glad you two are in the mates zone now. But, Mum?"

"Yes, Wes?"

"What *is* the friend zone then?"

Rorik smothered a laugh, and Poppy sent him a wry smile. "Why don't you tell him, smarty-pants?"

The knock on the door saved him from possible embarrassment. "Ah, our tea and food are here." He stood up.

"How about I explain another time? But, Wes, perhaps you could do your mother and me a favor?"

He cocked his head to the side. "What's that?"

"Don't ever ask Niklas for advice on women." With a wink at Poppy, he strode over to the front door.

After taking the tray and thanking the young maid who had brought the refreshments, he headed back into the living room. Wesley had now joined Poppy on the seat, cuddled to her side, and she stroked his hair as they watched the fire.

Rorik's dragon sighed in contentment as a warm, fuzzy feeling wrapped around his chest. And he realized right at that moment what the king had been trying to tell him.

That *this* was the point of it all.

EPILOGUE

Poppy wiped her damp palms down the front of her cardigan so many times, she was surprised her fingerprints hadn't rubbed off by now.

"Do not be nervous, my mate." Rorik slung his arm over her and squeezed her shoulder. "Everything will go splendidly."

"Not be nervous?" Was he joking? "How can I not be nervous when I'm about to meet your father?" She'd heard stories about the great Neils of House Asulf from the other Dragon Guard and the king. Some of them were comforting.

"It will be fine, and he will love you. Both of you," he assured her.

"Oh. Wes!" She glanced around her as they stood out in the lawn between the North Tower and the main palace hall, waiting for Rorik's father to arrive. "Where is he?"

"Probably still inside the library, but it's early yet. Father won't be here for another"—he checked his phone—"two minutes. He's always punctual. And Wesley knows to be here at precisely ten o'clock. Ah, there he is!"

EPILOGUE

Sure enough, Wes scampered out of the main building, books clutched in his hand as he made his way to them.

"Where have you been?" Poppy bent down and smoothed his tousled hair back.

"The newest *Adventures of Halfdan the Mighty* English translation just came out!" He held up the book excitedly at her. "It's not supposed to hit the stores until Monday, but Gideon got me copy."

She smiled wryly at him. Of course, he was almost late because of a book. *Oh, I hope you never change, Wes.*

"I still want to read the original, though, and I'm practicing every day. *Hei*, Rorik!" He said something else in Nordgensprak. She didn't understand whatever it was, but it made Rorik laugh.

"*Gut, gut,*" he said. "You are doing very well, Wesley."

He beamed at her. "Mum, there's something I want to tell you."

"What is it, Wes?"

"I ... I think I want to stay. Here, I mean. I want to keep going to school here in the Northern Isles. At least, for this year. If that's okay?"

Poppy could hardly keep the excitement from bursting out of her chest, but she had to stay calm. No matter how mature he seemed, she had to remind herself that Wesley was still very young. "If that's what you want, Wes. But we can apply for boarding school anytime if you change your mind. Anytime at all." She paused and bit her lip. "Is it your Dad? I promise you; he won't ever get to you." She looked up at Rorik and smiled. After all, thanks to him—and Gideon's special computer skills—they never had to worry about Robbie ever again.

EPILOGUE

As it turned out, the reason Mr. Grayford contacted Robbie first before he could file any petition in family court was because the solicitor had in his possession a certain video—the one Chablis had taken during the encounter at the park where his plans about exploiting Wesley and blackmailing Poppy could be clearly heard.

She didn't know the technical part of it, but Gideon explained that he found Chablis's social media accounts where she'd been posting photos and videos the entire afternoon. Though she'd deleted the video, Gideon somehow found a way to recover it and sent it to Mr. Grayford. He then showed it to Robbie and told him that if he attempted to sue for full custody or ever try to exploit Wesley, they would release the video. Needless to say, she hadn't heard from Robbie since.

"No, Mum." He clutched the book to his chest. "I like it here. I really do. This place feels like home now."

A snug, cozy warmth wrapped around her chest, and she knew it wasn't her own emotions she was feeling—it was her mate's. She didn't even have to look up at him to see that happy, content smile on his face.

The last couple of days had seemed like a dream. After her divorce, Poppy hadn't thought she'd find a partner again, at least not until Wesley was older. But this mating with Rorik was nothing like she'd ever felt before and perhaps never would again. Though their bonding was still new, it grew more and more every day. Wesley, too, warmed up to Rorik, albeit slowly, but she didn't push him or force him to show her mate affection. Rorik had asked her in private if Wesley still had any objection to their mating, but she told him to give him time.

EPILOGUE

"Look! He's here!"

Poppy got up and once again wiped away the sweat forming on her palms. Glancing up, she shielded her eyes from the sun with her hand and focused her gaze on a small dot on the horizon, which was rapidly turning into a large dot.

Despite having seen Rorik's dragon several times now, she was still awed by the sight of the fifty-foot winged creature. The dragon approaching was nearly identical to her mate's, but she did not feel the same fluttering in her stomach as she did each time she saw Rorik.

The dragon opened its mouth and let out a screech, then began its descent, lowering gently and smoothly transitioning to its human form, landing a few feet away from them.

"Father, welcome," Rorik greeted, stepping forward and opening his arms.

Neils of House Asulf looked like an older version of Rorik, with the same bright green eyes and hulking frame, though his red hair was liberally streaked with white. His massive arms spread as his son stepped into them, and they exchanged hearty hugs.

Wes gripped Poppy's hand tighter, and she gave him an encouraging squeeze. It seemed she wasn't the only one nervous about meeting Neils.

The two men faced each other silently, though Poppy could guess they were speaking telepathically. Niels looked over Rorik's shoulder. "Ah, this is your mate, then?" His accent was thicker than Rorik's.

"Yes." He stepped back. "Father, this is Poppy Baxter, my mate, and her son, Wesley."

She held out a hand. "Lovely to meet you—oh!" She

found herself pulled into a bear hug then lifted off her feet before being set down again.

Bright green eyes twinkled as he chuckled and planted his hands on his hips. "Ah, you are as lovely as the spring day in Fellstrond, Poppy. I am honored to meet you." His gaze lowered. "And young Wesley. An honor as well."

Wesley looked up at him in awe, and his grip on his book tightened. "N-nice to meet you. Sir."

His nose twitched, and he bent down. "I have heard much about you from my son. He says you are a smart young lad and—" His eyes narrowed. "Is that *Halfdan the Mighty*, Volume Four?"

"Y-yes, sir." Wesley's head bobbed up and down.

"Why, it's one of my favorite book series! Rorik loved it when he was little as well."

"I did?" Rorik frowned. "I don't remember ever reading them."

"No, your mother read them to you every night, before she passed." His mouth formed into a sad, wistful smile. "But, since I retired a few years ago, I started learning English and practiced my reading skills by reading English authors, though I always prefer the ones with action and adventure. Tolkien, for instance, was one of the first I read because I heard Forberg's works were influenced by him."

"That's exactly what I thought!" Wes's face lit up. "Gideon doesn't agree with me."

Neils tsked. "Wait until you get to volume twelve, when Halfdan encounters the elves of Dargaden."

Wesley's eyes went wide. "Have you read The Hobbit yet? That one's my favorite."

Neils let out a deep belly laugh. "Ah, yes. I'm afraid I'm

not too fond of his depiction of dragons in that one." He winked at Poppy. "The flight has left me famished. Son, do we have food ready?"

"Of course, Father. Let's head up to my apartments."

Brunch with his father turned out better than Rorik had expected. Of course, he knew Neils would certainly like Poppy, but it was a surprise that Wesley warmed up to him. He never thought of his father as the literary sort, but he supposed retirement could change anyone.

"I'm afraid we must leave soon," Rorik announced. "King Aleksei asked to see Poppy and me after our meal."

"Ah, yes. The new king. I have not seen him or Prince Harald since the coronation." His mouth pulled back into a thin line. "I'm only glad he survived that attack."

"Wesley, why don't you head back to our apartment, and I'll come back before dinner so we can get dressed?"

Neils glanced around. *Why are they not living with you, yet, son?*

We are taking things slow, Father, he replied. *It's only been a week since we bonded, plus, she wants to give Wesley time to adjust.* While he understood her reasoning and respected her decision, both he and his dragon were eager to have them both in their den. Plus, he longed to make slow, languid love to her all night long and wake up with her in his arms every day, instead of her having to go back to her apartment every night or snatching a few stolen moments with her when Wes was busy with homework.

Is she not certain she wants to be with you? Are you?

EPILOGUE

She is, believe me. He could feel it through their bond how much she loved and wanted him. *And so am I, otherwise I would not have asked you to bring the Asulf betrothal ring.* But he would wait for the right time to ask her to be his wife.

"Rorik?" Poppy lifted a brow at him. "Are you guys talking telepathically again?"

"Apologies, Poppy," Neils said. "It's quite rude of us."

"Ah, er, sorry," Rorik added. "Force of habit. Anyway, let's head out."

"Wait, I have an idea." Neils held up a hand. "Instead of young Wesley going back to your apartments, how about he come out and spend the day with me? I have no other plans."

Poppy hesitated. "I don't—"

"I guess that's fine," Wes said. "Maybe I can show you the library."

"Or I can show you the Cliffs of Despair on the northeast end of the palace grounds. It is my favorite place to fly."

Poppy let out a squeak. "Cliffs?"

"Father," Rorik warned. Wesley hadn't even asked him to fly him anywhere, and with his cheetah cub so anxious and skittish, it might take a while for him to trust his dragon.

"What?" Neils asked innocently. "Oh, all right, no cliffs. But, Poppy, may I ask your permission to spend time with Wesley?"

"I suppose that's all right with me. Are you sure you're okay with that, Wesley? You don't have to. Maybe you want to go back and read your book?"

"It's fine, Mum. I don't want to read too fast, or else it'll be over, and then I'll have to wait a whole year before the next translation comes out."

EPILOGUE

"All right, it's settled then," Neils said. "Go on, the boy and I will be fine."

After helping clean up, Rorik and Poppy headed to the residential wing of the palace, to the king and queen's apartments. Stein stood by the door and let them in.

The king is inside, he said.

Thank you, Stein.

Rorik wasn't sure exactly why the king and queen requested to see them both today, and in their home, too, instead of their offices. But it wasn't like they could say no. Perhaps they had questions about their mating and how it would affect their duties. While he was confident the royal couple wouldn't object, he would, of course, defend Poppy if he had to.

As soon as they entered, King Aleksei waved them over to the living area. "Ah, you're here. How was brunch with Neils?"

"It was good." He flashed Poppy a smile. She became more relaxed throughout the morning, and he was surprised that his father had seemingly mellowed out in the last few years. Or perhaps it was just Poppy, because surely anyone would be charmed by his mate.

"Have a seat." They did as the king bade. "Now, Poppy. I'd like to talk to you about your job."

"Oh!" She wrung her hands together. "I didn't realize ... but of course, our three months should be almost done by now."

"What? Oh yes, the probationary period. That's not why I asked you here."

"It's not?" she asked, puzzled. "Are you ... unsatisfied with my performance, Your Majesty?" He could feel the anxiety building in her. "Please, let me know what I can do to change your mind. I'll work harder and—"

"No, no, Poppy." He shook his head. "I'm not terminating your contract."

She breathed a sigh of relief. "Oh good."

"Er, actually I *am*. But I'm not firing you. I'm offering you another position."

"You are?"

"Yes. We will have an opening for a teaching position in the King Hakkonnen Elementary School next month. I'd like you to fill it."

"You do—I mean, me? Why?"

"You were a teacher before you came here, right? And Sybil tells me you're highly qualified and beloved by your former students. I think you would make a wonderful addition to the staff. Plus, I'm sure the hours would be better for you."

"I don't know what to say ..."

"Well? Do you accept? If not, then you can stay on as Alric's nanny, and we will extend your contract to two years."

"I ..." She looked to Rorik. "What do you think?"

"Me?" Her question caught him off guard. "It does not matter to me if you are a nanny or a teacher. You don't even have to work, if you want, and I will support you and Wesley." They would want for nothing. He would make sure of that.

"Oh, I couldn't do that." She took a deep breath. "I accept. Thank you, Your Majesty, I promise I won't let you down."

The king looked relieved. "Thank goodness. I really didn't know what to do if you had said no."

"You didn't?"

"Er ..." The king's expression turned serious. "Poppy, you have proved to us your capabilities, and because I trust Rorik with my life and my family's safety, I know I can trust his mate too."

"Of course you can, Your Majesty."

"Good. Because there's something I need to tell you. Both of you. There is—"

We're almost there, Queen Sybil said through their mind link. *Is the coast clear?*

Just Poppy and Rorik here, as we planned, the king answered.

Oh good. We're touching down in two seconds.

We? What did the queen mean by we?

"Looks like they got here just in time." The king rose to his feet, and Poppy and Rorik did the same.

There was a loud *whoosh* and *thud* that came from the direction of the balcony doors. A flash of gold glinted from the outside, and moments later, the double doors opened, and the queen strode in.

"I'm back," she said. "And I brought our guest." Stepping aside, she let someone in from behind her.

"Woo-hoo, that was fun!" The woman who casually strolled in behind Queen Sybil wore an all-black tracksuit and had a large backpack slung over her shoulder. "Reminds me of skydiving, with less falling. Thanks for the ride, Sybil. We should do it again sometime."

Sybil? Who was this woman who addressed the queen so casually? From the sound of her accent, she was American. His dragon immediately went on alert, as it always did when there were new people around the king and queen.

EPILOGUE

But there was something about this woman that felt different.

"Sure," the queen chuckled.

"Are you all right? No trouble during your trip?" King Aleksei asked. "Sit down, *lyubimaya moya* and have a rest."

"I'm fine, Aleksei, stop fussing. Poppy, you accepted the job, I hope?"

Poppy nodded. "Uh, yes ... but if you don't mind my asking, what is this about?"

"Oh, right." She gestured to the woman in black. "Everyone, this is Ginny. She's from the Blackstone Shifter Protection Agency."

"*You're* the undercover agent?" Rorik asked.

"Well, I won't be undercover for much longer if you shout it out like that." She marched over to him, hands on her hips, sky-blue eyes narrowing at him. "Or do you think that just because I'm a woman, I won't be able to find your mole? I've been doing this for years now, and I've never had my cover blown. Not even my family knows about my job."

Rorik's dragon reared its head as the woman came closer. *Shifter*. No wonder his dragon was on edge. But what was she? As he tuned into her, he sensed something fierce along with the scent of feline fur. "Apologies, I did not mean to imply that you were not capable. But, Your Majesty, I do not understand what Poppy has to do with this?"

"Remember how we were trying to find a suitable position for the undercover agent to take without arousing any suspicion? After much discussion, Sybil and I figured it out: She's going to replace Poppy as Alric's nanny."

"It's perfect, when you think about it," Queen Sybil said. "Poppy is our current nanny," the queen explained to Ginny.

EPILOGUE

"With her taking the teaching position, we'll have reason to train someone new. And that means Ginny will be able to move around the palace and amongst the staff without any suspicion."

"That makes sense," Poppy added. "No one really pays any attention to me, unless I'm with the prince."

"Of course, Poppy will stay to do her duties and pretend to train you," Queen Sybil added.

"That's great! Because I don't know shit about babies," Ginny chortled. "But don't worry, I shouldn't take too long. If you have a traitor in your midst here, then we can't waste any time. I'll sniff him out for you, lickety-split."

"It's settled then," the king said. "Rorik, please inform the rest of the guard of Ginny's presence so they can assist her in any way possible."

"Or just tell 'em to stay outta my way," she snorted. "I work better alone."

"I will, Your Majesty," Rorik said. "If that is all, we should take our leave and get back to my father and Wesley."

"Of course. We will see you at dinner tonight."

"Congratulations on the new job, Poppy!" Queen Sybil said.

"Thank you so much, Your Majesty," she replied. "I'll miss Alric terribly, though."

"You can visit him anytime," the queen assured her.

"I would very much enjoy that." Poppy curtseyed, and Rorik bowed to his king and queen before heading out.

"Congratulations," he said, placing his arm around her. "I have every faith you will do splendidly at your new job."

"I hope so," she said in a quiet voice. "I don't want to disappoint the king and queen. And the students. What if—"

"Poppy." He stopped and turned to face her, staring into her deep obsidian eyes. "Even without the presence of our 'guest,' I know Her Majesty would have recommended you for the position. You are an amazing teacher."

"I ... thank you."

"Anytime, my mate. Now, come. Let's see what trouble my father and Wesley might have gotten themselves into." As he led her down the hallway, he reached out to Niels. *Father?*

Done already?

Yes. It wasn't a long meeting. I'll tell you about it later. Now, where are you?

We are outside, by the reflecting pool.

"They're out in front," he said to Poppy.

Hand in hand, they made their way to the main hall and strode out of the palace. Though the reflecting pool area was of a considerable size, it wasn't difficult to spot Niels and Wesley. His great big hulking father was rolling around in the grass, laughing and howling as a small cheetah cub pounced and climbed all over him.

"Oh, dear." Poppy covered her hand with her mouth.

Rorik grumbled. "I can't believe him."

"Why, what's wrong?"

He huffed. "All he does is make Tolkien jokes throughout brunch, and now Wesley already adores him."

Poppy chuckled. "That one about not meddling in the affairs of dragons because 'you are small and delicious with mustard' made me laugh." Poppy squeezed his hand. "And for the record, Wesley likes you fine."

"He does?" He'd been worried because Wesley hadn't shown him affection yet. But he had to give the boy some time and space to adjust to the presence of another male in his mother's life. Besides, he would always protect Wesley and ensure his happiness, no matter what relationship they developed over time.

She nodded. "He told me the other night that he definitely hopes we stay in the mates zone."

He felt the corners of his mouth tug up. "If there is one thing you can be assured of, I will never let you out of the mates zone."

A loud splash made them both turn their heads at the same time. "Oh no," Rorik groaned. Somehow, Neils and Wesley managed to hop inside the reflecting pool and were now splashing about as they chased each other.

Rorik sighed and touched his forehead to hers. "Let us go and fetch that old fool before he embarrasses himself further."

She laughed aloud and gave him a quick peck on the lips. "They look like they're having fun, we should leave them be. Besides," she flashed him a cheeky grin, "we should take advantage now that Wes is occupied."

"What—oh, right." These moments alone had been too few and far between. His thoughts turned back to the ring sitting in his dresser drawer. Maybe he would make use of it sooner than later.

He slipped an arm around her waist and pulled her close. As he leaned down to press his mouth to hers, his dragon let out a sigh of contentment. His love for her seemed to grow exponentially every day, and it didn't seem like there was any limit. Sure, he still needed to work on finding that balance between being captain of the Dragon Guard and a mate, and some days were more challenging than most. For now, he was only certain of one thing: Poppy was his life, his heart, his reason for being.

"Take me away to your tower, my dragon," she said. "And make me yours."

"You *are* mine," he replied. "And I have always been yours."

Dear Reader,

Thanks for starting this adventure with me!

I hope you enjoyed Poppy and Rorik's story. If you want to read a hot, sexy bonus scene that happens right after the end:

http://aliciamontgomeryauthor.com/mailing-list/

You'll get access to ALL the bonus materials from all my books and my **FREE** novella **The Last Blackstone Dragon.**

But we've just begun and there's more love, romance, passion, and laughs.

Plus, a mystery (or three) to solve.

Who is the mole?

And is Ginny's fate waiting for her in the Northern Isles?

EPILOGUE

Find out in Dragon Guard Scholar!

Check out the preview on the next page.

Get it from your favorite online retailer.

Thanks again for reading!

All my love,

Alicia

PREVIEW: DRAGON GUARD SCHOLAR

Ginny Russel drummed her fingers on her arm as she stood on the edge of a barren cliff overlooking the Norwegian Sea. As she watched the icy water churn and listened to the surf breaking along the rocks below, her chest tightened as if gripped in an invisible vise.

Her inner lioness paced, perhaps sensing the activation of her flight-or-fight response. But how could she tell it that the perceived threat was all in her head?

She willed her animal to stay calm. As long as she stayed up here, she could manage the tension building up inside.

Taking deep breaths, she closed her eyes and envisioned soothing places, like the stillness of *Badain Jaran Dunes* of Mongolia or the *Salar de Uyuni* salt flats of Bolivia. Even thinking about the beautifully kept gardens of her childhood home in Colorado helped, despite the fact that she literally spent most of her adult life avoiding that place. When her body loosened up, she let out a sigh and her lioness lay down in a relaxed position.

Glancing down at her wristwatch, she checked the time.

Still early. It was a short hike from the sleepy little village where she'd stayed the previous evening. Before that, she'd taken three flights, driven six hours, and took ferry ride to get here. But in truth, she didn't mind the journey; that was the most exciting part of any trip for her. The exhilaration of travel never lessened even now, in the tenth year of her nomadic life.

However, hopping from place to place and country-to-country for a decade did have its downsides, namely, she'd gone to almost every place she wanted. Traveling began to get boring and for a while, she even thought it was time to settle down. In fact she nearly did; two and half years ago when she bought a one way ticket back home. And that's when things changed.

Her lioness suddenly went on alert, sending the hairs on the back of her neck bristling. It knew, before she could hear or see it, that something approached. Something *big*.

There.

Her enhanced shifter sight spied the small dot in the distance, becoming bigger as it drew closer. Her animal's ears pricked forward, then flattened out as its tail lowered. This time, Ginny knew what it was first. Or rather, who.

Her lioness cowered.

Calm down.

It hissed at her, as if saying, *you try calming down when there's a humongous predator up there.*

But this wasn't a predator, at least, not any normal predator. No, this creature rushing toward them was special. One of the few dragon shifters in the world.

As it drew closer, the golden scales that covered the dragon's gigantic body gleamed. Its giant horned head swung around, searching for something, until its gaze landed straight at Ginny, then made a long arc to re-direct its flight path. Leathery wings spread out, and it used the wind to glide, then slow down and descend toward the cliff.

She stepped back a few feet to give the dragon space as its clawed feet touched down on the rocky ground. The wind generated from its flapping wings nearly knocked her over, but she knew to dig in her heels to prevent from falling back.

The dragon began to shrink, its golden scaly body and giant horned head slowly disappearing until it was completely gone and only a dark-haired female stood in its place. "Hey, Ginny!" Sybil Lennox called as she slipped on the dress she had been carrying in her dragon's claws.

"What's up, Sybil?" she greeted back. "Long time no see."

Though Sybil Lennox was a few years younger than her, they'd known each other through their parents. Hank Lennox and Geraldine Russel had run in the same social and business circles, coming from two of the wealthiest and most influential shifter families in Colorado. Ginny recalled being invited to their castle for many birthday parties in her youth, and Sybil's older brothers Jason and Matthew had been in the same year as her brother Gabriel at Lucas Lennox High.

And now, apparently, she had married some king of a faraway land and ruled alongside him as queen. "Should I curtsy or bow, Your Majesty?"

Sybil approached, her silvery eyes rolling. "Ugh, no please. No formalities, at least not when we're alone. It's so nice to see you after all this time, Ginny! But, I have to admit I was surprised when Christina told me who she was sending to help us. I didn't even know you were part of The Agency."

"I'm the one they call on when they need someone to sniff out secrets," she said with a wink.

During that fateful trip back two-and-a-half years ago, an anti-shifter organization had planted bombs in what she considered her home town—Blackstone. When she heard about the trouble, she volunteered to help sweep for bombs. It was a dangerous task, but during the entire time there was an excitement and thrill she hadn't felt in years.

The town had been saved and in the aftermath, she discovered the existence of The Shifter Protection Agency or simply, The Agency, run by Sybil's brother Jason Lennox and his wife, Christina. They had been so impressed with her investigation skills that that brought her in as one of their recruits and after a solid year of training, started sending her out on missions.

Now when she traveled, she actually had a purpose. Though she'd done a variety of jobs for The Agency, undercover work seemed suited to her. Being pretty and petite helped, as few people suspected she had anything to hide, and putting on the dumb blonde act had gotten her out of more than a few scrapes. But she completed every mission assigned to her and nothing satisfied her more than bringing justice to the helpless and oppressed of her kind.

When it came to jobs, she was relentless and never stopped until she finished her mission then she moved onto the next. Her missions kept her grounded and in the present. Stopped her from dwelling on the past.

"Did Christina tell you what why we need help?" Sybil asked.

"Yes, she briefed me on the situation," she replied, grateful for the distraction. "You and your husband were attacked and you suspect someone on the inside had something to do with it."

"Yes." Sybil's nostrils flared and her eyes glowed briefly with the anger of her dragon. "We can give you more details when we get to the palace."

"Sure. When do leave?"

Sybil chuckled. "Now."

"Now?" Ginny glanced around. "But how ... oh." *Oh fuck.* Her stomach flipped like a pancake. They were flying to the palace—via Dragon Airlines, apparently.

"Are you alright?" Sybil cocked her head to the side. "You don't mind, do you? The Northern Isles doesn't have any commercial flights or ferries, and if we flew you in with the jet, we'd have to explain why you were there. Aleksei thought it would be better if there was no record of your arrival since we still don't who our mole is."

Ginny swallowed hard. "That makes sense. And no, it's no problem at all. I don't mind flying." No, flying wasn't the problem, after all. It was what was ahead, or rather, what they would be flying over.

The frigid, icy water stretching between them and their destination.

Her lioness backed away, snarling in displeasure, and Ginny couldn't even find the words to calm it down.

"Are you sure you're fine, Ginny? You look a little pale. I promise it's not a long flight. Just thirty minutes until we're over the main island."

"I'm sure," she said flatly, then turned on her heel to walk over to the rock where she had placed her backpack. "Ready when you are." Yet, the sweat beading on her forehead told her she'd never be ready. *As long as we fly high, I'll be fine.*

"Great. I'll grab onto you. I promise I won't let go."

"Thanks, I'm sure it'll be okay." It was *her* that was the problem, after all. With a deep breath, she secured to backpack her body. Sure enough, when she turned around, Sybil was gone and the dragon stood by the edge of the cliff. "Here goes nothing," she murmured under her breath.

Her lioness was calmer as they approached the dragon, perhaps sensing they were in no danger of being devoured by this particular predator. Its long, scaly arms stretched out and Ginny stepped forward into them. The limbs wrapped around her, and she found herself crushed against the surprisingly warm scales. She pressed her cheek against the leathery surface as she heard the flapping of wings and her feet lifted off the ground.

She held her breath as her heart and stomach suddenly felt like they were trying to switch places as the dragon soared higher and then dipped down. Her eyes shut tight as terror seeped into her veins. Thankfully, Sybil's dragon quickly found the perfect cruising altitude, and they moved forward at a steadier pace. Instead of thinking of what was below, she concentrated on the fact that she was *flying*.

Cracking one eye open, she turned her head and looked up. The sky was a perfect blue, and the puffy white clouds were so close she could probably hold her arms out and touch them. It was being in a plane, but so much better. The wind rushed around her, reminding her of skydiving in New Zealand, except she wasn't falling. It was exhilarating, and in this moment, she could forget all her troubles.

After what seemed like an eternity, they dipped low and began their descent. She plastered her body tighter against the dragon's chest, holding her breath until she heard a loud thump as the massive creature landed.

Her feet touched the ground and the dragon's grip loosened. The fact that could stand up straight without falling over was a miracle, as her knees were like jelly. But at least they were finally on solid ground and she didn't even see the ocean as they flew. However, the thought that they were surrounded by the sea set her on edge.

When Christina had told her about this assignment, she'd been eager for the challenge. Even after working non-stop for half a year now, she had no plans of slowing down, not when her work was the only thing keeping her distracted.

Heck, she had even been looking forward to visiting a new country. But that was before her research told her she would be living on an archipelago. The name Northern Isles should have given her a clue.

"Gosh, I really needed that." Sybil, now fully transformed and dressed, exclaimed. "I don't get to do much flying these days with my duties and all, plus Aleksei's being overprotective with me being pregnant and all."

"Oh, I didn't realize," Ginny said. "Congratulations."

"Thanks. Now, c'mon, let's head inside." They had landed on a huge balcony, and Sybil led her through the double doors that led into what Ginny assumed was Helgeskar Palace.

"I'm back," Sybil announced. "And I brought our guest." Stepping aside, she let Ginny in.

Now or never. Ginny put on her most confident air, hopefully to mask the maelstrom of emotions inside her. "Woohoo, that was fun!" she blustered. "Reminds me of skydiving, with less falling. Thanks for the ride, Sybil. We should do it again sometime."

"Sure," Sybil chuckled.

"Are you all right? No trouble during your trip?" A tall, handsome man with dark blonde hair strode forward, making his way to toward Sybil. While he looked harmless in his formal suit, Ginny's lioness cowed back, as it could tell he was the biggest and most dominant creature in the room. *So, this was the dragon king.* Intimidating was a mild word to describe him.

The king placed a hand on Sybil's shoulder. "Sit down, *lyubimaya moya.* You've had a long flight."

"I'm fine, Aleksei, stop fussing," she said, then glanced behind him. "Poppy, you accepted the job, I hope?"

Across what looked like the living room of a plush apartment was a brawny giant of a man and a small, pretty woman —Poppy—who nodded. "Uh, yes ... but if you don't mind my asking, what is this about?"

"Oh, right." Sybil gestured to Ginny. "Everyone, this is Ginny. She's from the Blackstone Shifter Protection Agency."

"You're the undercover agent?" the brawny giant asked. He was even bigger than the king, probably seven feet tall, with shoulders like rocks.

Ugh, of course. She should be used to the reaction by now, but it still irked her when people underestimated her because she was female. "Well, I won't be undercover for much longer if you shout it out like that." She marched over to him, hands on her hips. "Or do you think that just because I'm a woman, I'm can't find your mole? I've been doing this for years now, and I've never had my cover blown. Not even my family knows about my job." She could feel this man—dragon shifter—sizing her up, but she wasn't going to be intimidated.

"Apologies, I did not mean to imply that you were not capable." He turned to the king. "But, Your Majesty, I do not understand what Poppy has to do with this?"

"Remember how we were trying to find a suitable position for the undercover agent to take without arousing any suspicion? After much discussion, Sybil and I figured out it out: She's going to replace Poppy as Alric's nanny."

"It's perfect, when you think about it," Queen Sybil said. "Poppy is our current nanny," the queen explained to Ginny. "With her taking the teaching position, we'll have reason to train someone new. And that means Ginny will be able to move around the palace and amongst the staff without any suspicion."

"That makes sense," Poppy added. "No one really pays any attention to me, unless I'm with the prince."

"Of course, Poppy will stay to do her duties and pretend to train you," Queen Sybil added.

"That's great! Because I don't know shit about babies," Ginny chortled. "But don't worry, I shouldn't take too long. If you have a traitor in your midst here, then we can't waste any time. I'll sniff him out for you, lickety-split." She gave herself a week to solve this case. *Ten days, tops.*

"It's settled then," the king said. "Rorik, please inform the rest of the guard of Ginny's presence so they can assist her in any way possible."

"Or just tell 'em to stay outta my way," she snorted. "I work better alone." And it was better that way. Working alone meant she could make decisions on the fly without having to consult a partner. And if she was alone, no one else could get hurt.

After saying their goodbyes and the couple left the room, the king turned to Ginny. "I hope you are up to the task."

"I'll do my best, Your Majesty."

Sybil clapped her hands together. "Oh, sorry, I was so excited I didn't introduce you properly." She cleared her throat. "Aleksei, this is Ginny Russel. Ginny, this is my husband and mate, His Majesty, King Aleksei of the Northern Isles."

"Your Majesty." She bowed her head in deference. "An honor to meet you." That's what you said to royalty, right? She'd never met any king or queen in her life—well, not real ones anyway. She was pretty sure that guy with dreadlocks on that beach in Thailand wasn't a really royalty, even though he proclaimed himself king of the Phi Phi islands and invited her back to his palace/hut made of coconut palms.

"Ginny is actually from Blackstone and a friend of the family," Sybil continued. "You were in Jason and Matthew's graduating class, weren't you, Ginny?"

"My younger brother Gabriel was," she corrected. "I was in the year ahead."

"Ah, right," Sybil said.

"Miss Russel, thank you for coming on such short notice," King Aleksei said. "If there is anything we can do to assist your investigation, do let us know."

"Thank you, Your Majesty."

"But first, we must make the necessary preparations to keep your identity a secret."

"I've arranged for your apartments in the staff wing of the palace. It's not fancy, I'm afraid," Sybil said.

"I don't need to stay in a five-star hotel, I'm sure it's fine. Besides, it'll help me blend in better."

"You can use this day to get settled in," King Aleksei said. "I'll arrange for you to meet with the rest of the Dragon Guard first thing tomorrow."

"Dragon Guard?" she asked.

"They're kinda like our Secret Service," Sybil explained. "The man who was here with Poppy was their captain, Rorik."

"Oh right." *Oops. Maybe I should have been nicer to him if he was the head of security.*

"But let me call on one of them to escort you to your rooms," King Aleksei said. "Excuse me." He turned around and faced the windows.

"I'm going to call our head housekeeper to make sure everything's ready for you. Have a seat." Sybil led her to the living area, then walked over to the console table and picked up the phone. "This won't take too long."

"Awesome." Ginny dropped her backpack on the floor and plopped down on the plush couch.

Seconds later, the door opened, and a figure appeared in the entryway. "King Aleksei, I'm here."

Wow, that was fast. Ginny glanced behind her. The king didn't even move an inch from where he stood. How did he call this guy?

When the newcomer stepped inside, his gaze immediately landed on her. "Oh, hello," he greeted, a grin spreading over his face.

Oh, brother. She knew that look in his eyes, and she was *not* in the mood. Her lioness, on the other hand, eyed him warily, sensing another big predator in the room. *You're going to have to get used to that,* she told her animal. This was a land of dragons, after all.

He stalked over to her, his tall, lean body moving languidly like a cat. "I think I recognize you."

"You do, do you?" She crossed her arms over her chest and stared up at him. He was cute, she gave him that, though blond pretty boys weren't her usual type. Not that she had time to entertain any type these days.

"Uh-huh." He stared right back at her, amber eyes twinkling with amusement. "You look like my next girlfriend."

She burst out laughing because there was no way that was happening. "Oh my God, did you practice that in the mirror or something? Hmmm, I'd give you ... four out ten for effort."

To her surprise, her reaction didn't offend or anger him and instead, he chuckled. "All right then, let me try again." He cleared his throat. "What's your sign, baby?"

She rolled her eyes. "Dead End."

"Niklas!" Sybil admonished as she put the phone down. "Stop pestering Ginny."

"Er, sorry Your Majesty." He grinned at her again. "I have more where that came from."

"I don't want to know where those came from," she replied drolly, which earned her another laugh from Niklas.

"Well—Your Majesty." His face turned serious, and he bowed deeply.

King Aleksei walked up to them. "Niklas, this is Ginny Russel. She's the undercover agent The Agency sent to us to investigate the mole."

"Heya," she greeted.

The corners of his mouth quirked up as if he was trying

to stop himself from making some kind of smart remark. "Er, welcome, Ms. Russel. Let me know how I can be of service." The audacious man actually *winked* at her.

King Aleksei sent him a warning look. "If you don't mind, Niklas."

"Of course, Your Majesty. Right this way, Ms. Russel."

The queen looked at Niklas, one brow quirking up. He laughed and then bent down to pick up her backpack.

"Great." Ginny got to her feet. "I can carry that myself, thank you."

"Nah, it's fine." He waved her away. "C'mon, let's go."

He led her out of the suite, stopping briefly to nod at the statue standing right outside the door. A quick glance back told her that was no statue—but rather, another dragon shifter. He stood eerily still, steely eyes forward and jaw set. Something about him sent her lioness on the edge, but in a different way. Like it knew there was something not quite right about that other man.

"Don't worry about Stein," Niklas said. "That's just how he is. So," he glanced at her. "You're going to be the new nanny, huh?"

"I—wait a minute." She stopped and looked at him, then lowered her voice. "How did you know? I thought they didn't decide what my role would be until the previous nanny accepted her new job."

"The king told me," he said matter-of-factly.

"When?"

"He—oh!" He snapped his fingers. "I forgot, you're not from around here. As dragons of the same species, His Majesty and I can communicate via telepathy."

"Oh, no way? Really?" *Huh.* She'd never heard of any

other kind of shifter having that ability.

"Yeah." He wagged his eyebrows at her and leaned forward. "Wanna know what's on my mind?"

"Oh please." She placed a hand on his chest and pushed him away. "I don't think there's enough bleach in the world to clean my brain from the depraved thoughts lurking in there."

"I like you," he chuckled. "All right, all right, I'll stop. But first ... " He took a sniff of the air. "Hmm ... lioness, right?"

"Yes. How did you know?" Most shifters could narrow down another shifter's animal to species, but not exact animal.

"My first girlfriend was a lioness," he said. "Not an experience I'd care to repeat. You guys are vindictive."

"Only if you deserve it," she shot back. "And I'm guessing you did."

"Probably." He flashed her a boyish grin then cocked his head. "C'mon, let's keep going."

She followed him down the long, luxuriously decorated hallway, then down a set of stairs. The palace must be huge because it took them another fifteen minutes of walking before they reached what she deduced was the staff wing of the palace. It was located on the ground floor, past the kitchens, and the corridors here were more utilitarian and modest. Niklas seemed to know almost everyone and greeted them as they passed by, then led her into one of the offices where he introduced her to the head housekeeper, a middle-aged woman named Mrs. Anna Larsen.

"The nannies usually stay closer to the royal apartments for convenience, but Her Majesty told me that you would be staying in the staff wing until you fully transition into your position," Mrs. Larsen said.

"I should get going," Niklas said. "But Their Majesties requested that I give you a tour of the palace. Let's meet at the main foyer at five, if that's okay?"

She took her backpack from him. "Sounds great. See you, Niklas."

"Can't wait." He winked at her, then turned on his heel and walked in the opposite direction.

"Come this way, Ms. Russel," Mrs. Larsen said. "I'll show you to your room."

They headed down a long hallway, then stopped at the fourth door on the left. "Here you go, Ms. Russel. It's an ensuite so you should have everything you need and the staff dining room is open twenty-four hours a day. You are welcome to eat as much as you like, plus you're free to make your own meals as well with the ingredients we stock in the pantry. If you need anything, just let me know."

"Thank you Mrs. Larsen."

"Welcome to Helgeskar Palace." With a nod, she left.

"Alrighty then." Ginny squared her shoulders and walked inside. "Huh." The room was larger and more comfortable than she'd imagine for staff housing. There was a double bed in the corner, a large window with a view of the outside, a desk, flatscreen TV, and wardrobe. Setting her bag down on the floor, she walked over to the bed and sat down, then lay back.

She let out a long sigh. *Another day, another, another mission*. But this is what she signed up for, after all. It was bright and sunny outside, but despite the traveling and jet lag, she wasn't tired. She was a shifter, after all, and didn't need as much rest as normal humans. And she didn't sleep.

Not anymore. Not when the darkness of sleep only brought on nightmares she'd sooner forget.

Getting up, she reached for her backpack. She had a couple of hours before she had to meet Niklas, so she needed to get to work. Unpack, reach out to HQ, then figure out how to hunt for a traitor who aided in the assassination of a king. *Easy peasy.*

" ... and you're doing well so far?" Christina Lennox asked, her voice tinny through the small speakers of the beat-up laptop. "No problems?"

"Yup, all good so far." Ginny had to wait until it was morning in Colorado to call her boss via video chat, which was around four o'clock in the afternoon, Northern Isles local time. "The king said he'll arrange for me to meet his security team tomorrow and give me a more comprehensive view of the situation." She wished it was sooner, but she supposed one more night couldn't hurt.

"Excellent."

"I'll find this mole lickety-split, don't you worry." This wasn't just any normal case, after all, and not just because the dragons were one of The Agency's most powerful allies. This was personal for Christina, as Sybil was her sister-in-law.

"I know you will, otherwise I wouldn't have assigned this case to you," Christina said. "Thanks for hopping right on it."

"Just have my next assignment ready."

Christina's brows drew together. "About that ... Ginny, don't you think it's time for a break? You've been working nonstop. Maybe you should slow down."

Ginny stiffened. "I don't need a break."

"That's what you keep saying." Christina's expression turned worrisome. "It's been almost six months since Malta. I know it's been tough, but Kristos—"

"I said, I don't need a break," she snapped. "Sorry, I have to go meet someone soon. Bye Christina, I'll update you as soon as I wrap things up here." She quickly slammed the laptop lid down and shut her eyes tight. Her chest tightened and her lungs were collapsing in. Like they did *that* day, when they were filling with saltwater.

It was *everywhere*. Around her. Over her head. Smothering her like a cloak and—

Her lioness growled, knocking her out of the memory, and she could breathe again.

It had felt so real. Like it was happening again. She raked her hands through her hair, her hands still shaking.

Can't dwell on it. Need to forget. She forbade herself from thinking about that incident. It was ancient history, and she didn't need to remember anything about it.

Except Kristos.

When was the last time anyone mentioned that name around her? Or even heard it aloud?

His funeral, probably.

An ache in her chest bloomed and her lioness mewled in a comforting manner. Counting to ten, unclenched her jaw. *It's fine. I'm fine,* she told her animal. Her eyes darted to the clock on the bedside. "Shit!" It was five minutes to five, and she still had to find her way through the maze-like corridors of the palace and out to the main foyer. How long had she been in a daze?

Dashing out of the room, she did her best to retrace her

steps out of the staff wing. But once she reached the main palace, everything looked the same. *Did we turn left or right at the painting of the guy riding a horse? Or was it the other guy on the horse?* Dammnit, she was already late.

Unsure what else to do, she turned the next corner. However, she bumped into someone rushing in the other direction, sending her scrambling backwards. "Oh shit! I'm sorry!" She steadied herself. "My bad! I wasn't looking—" Ginny blinked and found herself staring into familiar amber eyes. "I ..." She gasped. *Niklas?*

Mine, her lioness roared.

And something big and fierce shrieked it right back.

Niklas's mouth parted, but nothing came out. He just stood there, amber gaze boring into her.

No, he couldn't be—

But her lioness repeated it again. *Mine.*

Niklas was her mate.

A surge of panic rose up in her. And this time, she let her flight response take over. Using her shifter speed, she ran past him, then turned into the first hallway on the right, then into the next. When she decided she was far away enough, she slowed her pace, but kept on walking.

Her heart beat like mad in her chest, threatening to escape. How could Niklas be her mate? They met this morning and her animal didn't say anything. Was it a delayed response?

Not every shifter had a mate. In fact, many shifter couples had successful marriages even without the mating bond, like her parents. But when her brother Gabriel had met his mate Temperance, he said that he knew right away, the moment he looked into her eyes.

Maybe I'm too broken.

Her animal shook her head. *Mine,* it repeated.

Oh God. A mate? Her? It couldn't be. She didn't need a mate right now. Or ever. Certainly not a dragon. Plus, she could never live here. Or in any one place. It would drive her mad. She needed her freedom to roam and travel.

Okay, calm down, she told herself. Maybe Niklas didn't want a mate either. Sure, he was flirty and all, but she could tell he was a player, with all those cheesy lines. Plus, he looked about as shocked as she had been.

Taking a deep, cleansing breath, she straightened herself and turned around. In her mad dash to get away from Niklas, she had somehow found herself in a familiar hallway. She'd definitely seen that statue of the man playing the flute this morning. *And that rug with the blue squiggles.* All she had to do was turn right at the end and—

"Ah-ha!" she exclaimed when she saw the long winding staircase that led to the staff apartments. At least now she could go back to her room and figure out what to do.

"Ginny?"

She stopped short at the sound of the familiar voice behind her. *Shit.* "Hey Niklas," she began. "We should probably talk."

"Talk?"

Pursing her lips together, she turned around to face him. "Yeah. About what happened."

"What happened?"

She frowned. "You know. I—" *Wait a minute.* Narrowing her gaze, she peered up at his face. Those amber eyes peered back at her and ...

Nothing.

Huh?

Not a peep from her lioness nor from his dragon.

What the hell?

"Ginny?" He waved a hand in front of her face. "What's going on? You okay? Do you need a minute?"

More like a lifetime. "Uhm, no, I'm fine. I just ... got a little lost."

"Oh." He scratched at this chin. "Yeah when you didn't show up, I figured you must have taken a wrong turn or something. Do you want to do the tour another time? We could just grab dinner."

"What? No, I'm great. Fine. Dandy." She blew out an annoyed breath. Wasn't he going to say anything about what happened earlier?

"Oh cool. All right," he began. " Why don't I start by orienting you so you can find your bearings?"

"That sound great." Well, if he wasn't going to say anything, she wasn't going to either. Besides, what was she supposed to tell him? *Sorry I freaked out, but I hallucinated you were my mate.*

Inwardly, relief poured through her. No, the last thing she needed was a freaking dragon mate. Her animal, on the other hand, sat in the corner and pouted.

Ugh, weirdo. Maybe being out here was affecting her shifter side. In any case, that was another reason to finish this mission quickly and get the hell out of the Northern Isles.

Dragon Guard Scholar: Dragon Guard of the Northern Isles Book 2 is available from your favorite online retailer.
Get it now!

ABOUT THE AUTHOR

Alicia Montgomery has always dreamed of becoming a romance novel writer. She started writing down her stories in now long-forgotten diaries and notebooks, never thinking that her dream would come true. After taking the well-worn path to a stable career, she is now plunging into the world of self-publishing.

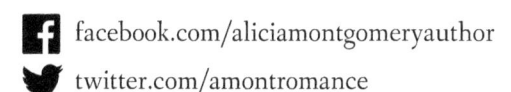

- facebook.com/aliciamontgomeryauthor
- twitter.com/amontromance
- bookbub.com/authors/alicia-montgomery